SIMPLY WONDERFUL

Daisy joined Kenneth in the living room. He sat in a soft chair across from her. The large rectangle table stood between them.

This meeting was strictly business. She felt that, like her, the rest of the world held its breath in suspense to learn the secrets of Kenneth's identity.

There was the truth to discuss, perhaps even their future.

Daisy's voice was soft. "Tell me who you are."

"My name is Kenneth Steven Gunn. I'm in my thirties. Single. No children. No special woman in my life. I live alone in a condo in Wichita, Kansas. I'm a private investigator in business for myself."

So far so good, she reasoned. His instincts about the kind of man he figured himself to be had proven correct. From the beginning he believed he was the type of man who would stay loyal to the woman he loved, the kind of man who would proudly wear his wedding ring if he had one.

Daisy was glad because he had kissed her. She was glad because she had enjoyed being in his arms. Now that the time had come for Kenneth to leave her, she didn't want him to go.

SIMPLY WONDERFUL

Shelby Lewis

BET Publications, LLC
www.bet.com
www.arabesquebooks.com

ARABESQUE BOOKS are published by

BET Publications, LLC
c/o BET BOOKS
One BET Plaza
1900 W Place NE
Washington, D.C. 20018-1211

All Kensington Titles, Imprints, and Distributed Lines are available at special quantity discounts for bulk purchases for sales promotions, premiums, fund-raising, educational, or institutional use.

Special book excerpts or customized printings can also be created to fit specific needs. For details, write or phone the office of the Kensington special sales manager: Kensington Publishing Corp., 850 Third Avenue, New York, NY 10022, attn: Special Sales Department, Phone: 1-800-221-2647.

First Printing: December, 2000

10 9 8 7 6 5 4 3 2 1
Printed in the United States of America

For my sister, Toni . . . may your own wildest dreams come true. Lots of love, Shelby.

A NOTE FROM THE AUTHOR

What is a rose nursery and garden shop?

A rose nursery and garden shop is a place where plants are raised for sale and for exhibition. It is a place where seasoned gardeners and neophytes gather to learn more about the world's favorite flower, to trade its growing secrets, and to enjoy the pure beauty of scent, shape, and color in a plant that has thrived nearly forty million years on this planet. Regardless of how flawless the garden, there is always room for a few surprises. . . .

One

A late-model black Impala cruised the seventy miles-per-hour speed limit on Interstate 35 heading north to Wichita, Kansas. The driver, a short bodybuilder with two gold front teeth, said to his partner in crime, "We gotta get rid of him."

"Yeah."

The accomplice was only an inch taller than the bodybuilder, who was exactly five feet two inches tall. The major difference between them was that the partner in crime was so skinny, the seat of his pants sagged and the waistband of his thirty inch-by-thirty inch Wrangler jeans had room to spare. His stomach growled. "I'm ready to eat."

"Man, I don't know how you do it."

"High metabolism."

The bodybuilder swore under his breath. "You ain't lying. If I didn't pump iron, I'd be the Pillsbury Doughboy. But you, ha! You can eat whatever you wanna eat, whenever you wanna eat it, and your pants still hang off your butt. It just ain't right."

The skinny man looked at the prone male body beside him. He was their victim for the night. "It'll take us both to unload this dude. There's no telling how long he'll be knocked out. I say we either kill him now or dump him now."

The bodybuilder squinted his eyes in order to read the upcoming road sign. The sign read, GUTHRIE, NEXT 2 EXITS. "Boss said, beat 'em up and dump 'em. Didn't say nothing about killing."

"Then Guthrie it is."

The black Impala with the dark tinted windows on all four sides and the stolen license plate turned west off Interstate 35 onto Highway 77. The car passed the Vance Auto Dealership on the right. On the left, the Impala passed a car lot filled with used vehicles offered by the auto dealer, Jim Miles. There were no streetlights on the two-lane highway.

The bodybuilder was pleased with the way things were going for him and his friend. "Man, this is perfect."

"Yeah. Pull over."

The black Impala, with its quiet motor and its dark metal body, glided to a stop in front of Daisy's Rose and Garden Shop. It was three A.M. The bodybuilder depressed the button for the driver's-side window. Once the window was all the way down, he angled his head through the open space. The air felt cool, mild, absolutely refreshing.

The only thing stirring in the vicinity of the Impala was a white-horned owl on the hunt in the night. The seasoned hunter glided on the breeze under a full moon with a wingspan broad enough to cast a shadow on the ground.

The bird spied the glowing dashboard instruments inside the sleek Chevy. It's response to the eerie glow was, "Hoo, hoo," the sound low, deep, nearly human in pitch.

The bodybuilder registered the sound. It caused him to shiver a little in his gray-and-black boa constrictor boots. "Man, that owl sounds creepy."

"Yeah."

"Let's get moving."

"Sho', you right."

The skinny man opened the rear passenger door behind the driver's seat. Using both hands, he gripped the unconscious passenger beneath his armpits and pulled. Nothing. He pulled harder. The passenger scarcely budged an inch.

"I say we kill him and ditch the car."

"That's not what the boss said."

"Forget the boss."

"Not in this life." The bodybuilder hefted his bulk from behind the leather-wrapped steering wheel. Outside the car, he flexed his fingers, rolled his shoulders, and lolled his head from side to side until the stem of his neck popped. "Let a pro handle it, bro. We ain't got all night."

The skinny man stepped aside. "Be my guest."

The bodybuilder opened the rear passenger door. He lifted the prone man's feet from the floor of the car. He pulled and he pulled, but only two inches of dead weight cleared the distance from the backseat of the car to the gravel on the ground in front of Daisy's Rose and Garden Shop.

The frustrated bodybuilder stepped to the right of his snickering friend. "Okay, man. Let's get this show on the road. I'm kinda hungry, too."

"Yeah."

Working together, the lawbreaking friends hauled the prone man out of the rear seat of the idling Impala. The victim hit the ground with a solid thump. The skinny man dropped the left foot he carried in order to return to his original position at the head of the victim. He grabbed the man under the arms, then lifted the top half of the limp body.

The bodybuilder retained his position at the victim's feet, feet with size twelve basketball shoes still laced and firmly in place. The unconscious man's butt scraped the gravel on the ground of the parking lot as the stealthy criminals sought a place to stash him long enough for them to get from Guthrie, Oklahoma, to Wichita, Kansas, before sunup.

The bodybuilder noticed piles of what looked like crumbly dirt and unknown debris. He jerked his smooth shaved head to the left, in the direction of a greenhouse that stood just under four feet tall. "Over there."

To the right of the greenhouse, a small glass structure with metal shelves scattered with start-up plants, were three large dark piles. The straining men dumped their victim into the pile nearest the house of glass.

The skinny man hooked his thumbs in the belt loops of his waistband, hitched up his Wranglers, then cocked a thumb at the cool dark pile of . . . debris. He leaned his body toward the pile, pinched a sample of the unknown matter with his fingertips, brought the sample to his twice broken nose, and sniffed. He wasn't sure what he smelled. "What is this mess anyway?"

The bodybuilder stomped his boa constrictor boots on the gravel four times before he realized what he was doing. It was quiet at three A.M., way too quiet to make unnecessary noise. The sound of hard-soled boots stomping the ground was as distinctive a sound as a white-horned owl chanting, "Hoo, hoo," into a night growing shorter by the second.

The lawbreaking men didn't have time to smell the dirt . . . or the roses. "Man," he said, "we betta split."

"Yeah."

They were gone in sixty seconds.

The victim woke to a taste in his mouth he couldn't even begin to identify. The substance was cool, damp, and nothing to write home about. He spit the grit from his mouth as he tried to figure out why he felt so bad.

His forehead felt as if somebody had used it for target practice. The balls of his eyes burned the backs of his lids. To his dismay, his lashes were dusted with the same foreign substance he had spit from his mouth. He wanted a shower so bad, he could hear the water running in his mind.

He shook his head at the foolish thought, then regretted the shaking action when his head felt as if his brains were rolling around like a dozen cat's-eye marbles. He had to get onto his feet, out of the mystery pile, and into reality.

His number-one priority, getting onto his feet, was also his number-one problem. His entire body felt like an overused cushion at the bottom of a high-jump bar: totally trounced and ready to bust at the seams. He just had to get up.

Had to.

Grunting with effort, the victim rolled to his right side. He forced himself onto his right knee. Resting his right forearm on his right knee, he worked at catching his ragged breath. Whatever was wrong with him, it flat out wasn't good.

His chest felt kicked in and broken down. His head was

spinning. When he felt around on his face with his fingers, he realized his right eye was swollen and both his lips were cut. Whoever had worked him over had worked him down to the bone.

The victim felt as if the very insides of his bones were crying with pain and agony. He had to get help, had to get on his feet, out of the mystery pile, and into . . . first, he had to get on his feet.

He felt around for something sturdy to latch onto with his sore, swollen hands. He found nothing. If he got on his feet at all, he'd have to do it with willpower. He glanced at the watch strapped to his left wrist. The glow-in-the-dark sports dial read 3:40 A.M. It was too dim around him to see more than two feet away from the mystery pile.

What a mess.

Since he didn't know where he was, he didn't want to holler for help. There was no way to tell what kind of danger lurked in the shadows of the buildings around him. He didn't have the strength to fight. Judging by the soreness of his hands, both of them cut up and encrusted with what he figured to be dried blood, he decided that he'd done enough fighting for one day—or two.

Willpower.

That's what he needed.

Willpower, and plenty of it.

This time, when the victim struggled to his feet, he managed to stay up. He took five staggering steps forward, then two staggering steps to the left before he felt like throwing up.

His chest hurt so bad he wished he could disconnect it from the rest of his body. His entire body was crying out for the kind of serious painkiller only a medical doctor could prescribe.

That's what he needed: a doctor.

The victim decided he'd better take his chances with the danger lurking inside the shadows of the buildings around him to go after some help. If anybody needed rescue from a Good Samaritan, it was definitely him.

With his left eye open and his right eye swollen closed, he staggered his way a couple of feet from the mystery pile and straight into the glass greenhouse. Some part of his rattled brain registered that the structure he'd stumbled into was small, no more than four feet tall, three feet wide, which is precisely why the whole thing came tumbling down when he lost his precarious balance.

Grunting with pain, flat on his back, the miniature glass house on top of his badly bruised chest, he lost his battle to find reality; once again, he was unconscious. The last thing he remembered was the cool, damp feel of the mystery pile against the skin on the back of his neck, the sight of something big casting its shadow against the ground, and the smell of roses. He loved the smell of roses.

Daisy Rogers heard the crash of the glass greenhouse and knew right away that something was more than a little wrong. Not in the least bit cautious, she threw on her sweatpants, stuffed her feet into a pair of green rubber garden clogs, and marched out of the house with a flashlight. The flashlight was heavy duty, its gleam reaching far and wide.

It shocked her to see the long form of a fallen man lying in the middle of one of her compost piles. Her first instinct was to run. She was alone. It was almost four o'clock on a Friday morning. There was a man in her garden, a man big enough to knock her miniature greenhouse to the ground.

She could run to the house, lock herself inside, and call the Guthrie Police Department . . . but the man hadn't moved an inch since her arrival. A man that big with a light shining down on him and a weighted glass piled on top of his chest had to be hurt. When he didn't move for another two minutes, Daisy decided she would hold off on the local police and see if she could help the stranger herself.

She wouldn't be crazy. She would help the man but she would get her dog to play backup first. Daisy's dog was a seventy-five-pound German shepherd named Cutie Pie. If something went wrong, Cutie Pie would take care of it, no special command required.

Just thinking about the German shepherd had a calming effect. Cutie Pie was sweet on the inside, warm, friendly, and downright cuddly unless she thought Daisy was in any sort of jeopardy.

By the tone of the whistle Daisy used to summon Cutie Pie, it took less than a moment for the shepherd to recognize the heightened tension in her owner's manner and to respond accordingly.

The muscular shepherd emerged from her house with her ears pricked up, her coarse black and tan fur slightly on end, her heavy tail high and tight, the tip curled scorpion-style. Whatever was up, Cutie Pie was ready.

Daisy left her dog off the leash so the shepherd would have total freedom to do whatever she felt she had to do to keep the stranger in line. Daisy grabbed her cell phone in her left hand, keeping her flashlight in her right hand. She was ready, too.

Cutie Pie ran straight to the fallen man. She sniffed his prone body while Daisy struggled to move the greenhouse. The going was tough. The greenhouse wouldn't budge. She tried to pull the man from beneath the glass structure after she put down her cell phone and flashlight. That was tough, too.

In the end, she decided the injured man was too heavy to be pulled. She checked his pulse. It was strong. She checked the rest of him out. His face was jacked up. His clothes were clean, his body fit. With Cutie Pie there, Daisy felt confident.

The stranger had no weapon she could find, a fact that reinforced her decision to help him. The way Daisy had things figured, the stranger was on her turf, which was quite all right under the odd set of circumstances. It was all right because of Cutie Pie. Cutie Pie was the equalizer.

Daisy braced her feet and set to work. She began to unload the contents from inside the greenhouse in order to make it light enough to pull off the injured man. Out came the peat pots, the bag of vermiculite, the Schultz potting soil, the root starter solution, the plastic plant identity markers, the Magic markers, and the new plants themselves.

In minutes, the greenhouse was lighter. Daisy put her shoulder to the broad side of the miniature building. She braced her feet. She shoved. The greenhouse began to move. But so did the stranger.

Getting the greenhouse partially off his chest helped him to breathe easier, which in turn helped him to wake up. Daisy didn't know if it was true or not, but she thought it made perfect sense.

The stranger groaned.

Cutie Pie growled in response.

Daisy stopped shoving the greenhouse in order to lay a calming hand on Cutie Pie's neck. "Down, girl."

Cutie Pie went quiet, but her hackles stayed up. Her muscles were tight, ready for any type of action.

The stranger opened his eyes.

Daisy adjusted the flashlight so that she could see the stranger better. He definitely looked as if he'd received the wrong end of somebody's stick. "I'm glad you're awake," she said. "It'll take us both to get this thing off your chest. On the count of three, let's shove this sucker to your right."

He said, "One."

She said, "Two."

Together they said, "Three." The greenhouse slid over to the right of the stranger in one motion.

Daisy got down on her haunches. "Can you stand?"

"Not without help."

She braced herself for leverage. "Come on. On the count of three I want you to stand up. One. Two. Three!"

It took a full minute, but they got him on his feet. Cutie Pie immediately began sniffing the stranger in earnest. He stood totally still while she did it, as if aware that the next few moments regarding his safety had more to do with Cutie Pie's comfort zone than it did her owner's. After another minute, Cutie Pie stepped back.

Daisy took this as a positive sign. She trusted Cutie Pie's instincts as much as she trusted her own. Her instincts told her to give the stranger the benefit of the doubt by considering him a victim of some sort of violence rather than a potential enemy. "Come on. Let's get you into the house."

He groaned.

For some reason, she understood that groan. "I know, it's a long way to the house. We'll take it easy. I'm not in a rush."

Daisy retrieved the flashlight, which the stranger took from her hands in order to light the way. Slowly, he limped while she half dragged him the fifty yards between the compost pile and the back door of her bungalow.

He leaned on her so hard, Daisy's shoulder felt as if a sack of potatoes had landed on it. "God, you're heavy."

"Sorry."

"Save your breath, mister. You're gonna need your strength to get up the steps to the house."

He groaned some more.

Despite the severity of the moment, Daisy laughed. "What a way to watch the sun come up, hey?"

Other than the impression she was physically small, the stranger noticed his rescuer had a beautiful voice. It was light, clear, like clean water running off the eaves of a house after a hard rain.

Curious, the stranger stopped limping forward so that he could look down at the Good Samaritan of his dreams. Definitely, she was not a figment of his imagination. Her hair was wrapped in a red bandanna, and she had on gray sweats that, even in the dim light, he could tell were smudged with the gritty substance he had fallen into and that she'd hauled him out of. Her eyes smiled at him as if he were a stray puppy she had found hurt in her garden instead of a strange man.

How could one man be so lucky? The injured man shook his head in wonder at his rescuer's trusting ways. The instant he shook his head, he felt dizzy again. The swimming sensation in his head caused him to sway on his feet.

"Take it easy, big fella," she counseled. "If you fall down now, we both fall down. We'd really be in trouble then."

Up the steps the couple went, Cutie Pie right behind them. Inside the kitchen, Daisy kicked a chair out from under the table, a circular wood table inlaid with country blue ceramic tile.

Groaning in relief that his brief but painful journey from the yard to the house was over, the stranger fell onto the chair Daisy provided out of the goodness of her heart. Exhausted, he let his head loll to the left side.

Daisy flipped the white light above the table to the on position. Her guest blinked from the unexpected brightness. She checked him out in detail. "Nice eyes. Brown with green flecks. At least the one that's still open looks nice. Whoever worked you over didn't leave too much of your face untouched."

"Water," he croaked.

"Coming right up." Daisy's water was pumped from a fresh water well in the backyard into the house. She ran the water cold from the kitchen tap into a short clear glass decorated with apple blossoms.

The stranger took a sip. The water soothed his throat, washed away the grit from his mouth. A glass of water never tasted so good. "Thank you."

"No problem. I see your hands are pretty shaky." She took the cup from him. "I'll get some hot water and towels to get you cleaned up. You may need to go to the hospital. There's one not too far from my place that I can take you to."

The stranger reached a hand toward Daisy's face, as if to make triple sure she was a living woman and not a figment of his desperate imagination. Before he passed out, he'd been praying for a Good Samaritan to rescue him.

This woman, dressed in practical rubber clogs and sweats wasn't a mirage . . . she was a miracle. The light was on. The chair was hard. This was for real. Real. Thank God. The stranger's intense look alarmed Cutie Pie.

The shepherd growled low in her throat.

At the sound of the dog's displeasure, the stranger stopped moving his hand midair. He needed his fingers.

Daisy said, "It's all right, Cutie Pie. Sit."

Cutie Pie sat. But it was clear she didn't want to sit. She kept one unblinking eye on the stranger, who kept one unblinking eye on her.

To the stranger, Daisy said, "Let's get you cleaned up."

He nodded his head once in agreement, his expression closed but watchful. There was a single cup on the cream Formica counter. One dinner plate with the flaky edge of a pie crust still on it. One silver fork. The lack of multiple cups, plates, and eating utensils didn't mean she lived alone, but they were strong clues to the stranger that she probably did.

Her seclusion increased the value of the gifts she presented him—with her caring hands and her gracious time. She could easily have called the police to rouse him from her garden and oust him off her property. Instead of adding fuel to the fire of his arrival, she chose to add hope. For this, the stranger would forever be thankful.

Wanting to pick up more clues about the Good Samaritan's personality, he scanned the kitchen. There was nothing splashy about the comfortable room. There was plenty of storage in the form of wall cabinets, their white veneers clean with a high-gloss shine.

There was a center cooking island with a convenience sink. The cabinets on the island where also white. In the open slots and spaces of the island were cookbooks and small pots of live green plants. It was a working kitchen, versatile in its utility.

Daisy didn't take long to return to the kitchen with fresh peach-colored towels, antiseptic, bandages, and a pair of plastic gloves. She then set to work healing the stranger. She began her first-aid routine by filling a bowl with warm water from the kitchen sink. "This is gonna hurt you a whole lot more than it's gonna hurt me."

He blinked twice before saying, "Go ahead."

She started with his face. Gently, she pressed her fingers over his flesh to feel for shattered bones. There were none. She removed the blood from his face. She applied antiseptic but paused in sympathy when he hissed at the sting.

"Like I said," she reminded, "this is gonna hurt you a whole lot more than it's gonna hurt me."

"Keep going." He spoke through clenched teeth.

Daisy took first one hand and then the other into her own. She cleaned his knuckles thoroughly to avoid infection. She didn't put any bandages on him so that he would have full use of his hands.

She went to the freezer and removed an ice pack. She

wrapped the ice pack in a dish towel and put it in his right hand. "Keep this on your swollen eye. It looks awful."

He smiled. It was crooked and appeared painful to make, yet the stranger's smile was genuine.

Daisy's voice was grave. "You're one lucky guy. If you had ended up two houses down, Miss Culpepper would have shot you first and asked questions later. She's sixty-three and still breaking horses."

The stranger started to laugh, but gripped his chest in pain instead. He wouldn't completely recover from his multiple injuries anytime soon.

Daisy's heart went out to him. "I'm gonna unbutton your shirt. The way you were moving on the way to the house from the garden had more to do with your upper body than with your legs. On top of that, you're breathing sounded labored. I think you might have a few busted ribs."

"Hope not."

"Me too. Let's take a look."

This time, it was she who groaned. "I'm in way over my head here. You should have X rays."

"I'm probably just bruised."

"Maybe. The trouble is, you're just about bruised everywhere I can see, even on your stomach. I'd feel better if a doctor looked at you. Besides, the way you were knocked out, I'd say you've suffered a concussion. So, if it's okay with you, I'd like to get you to the ER for a quick look. It shouldn't take too long for you to be seen because it's still early in the day. What do you say?"

He paused as if to consider his options. At the moment, they were limited. "I'm ready." Some of the tension left his shoulders.

"Good." Daisy visibly relaxed. "I don't think I want to risk those stairs again without some help. I doubt you need an ambulance, but we do need some muscle to haul you out of here. I'm gonna call my friend, Chester Whitcomb. It won't take a minute."

She started over to the phone on the wall. She paused, then looked back. "By the way, my name's Daisy. Daisy Rogers." She studied him intently, her manner expectant, her eyes bright. When he didn't respond, she prodded him. "And your name is . . . ?"

His sigh was long, heartfelt, and totally disgusted. "Lady," he said, a scowl on his jacked-up face, "I have no idea."

Daisy hiked her left brow at him. "You've gotta be kidding."

"No. It's the truth."

She opened her mouth, then closed it again. First she'd heard a bump in the night. Second she'd found a strange man in her compost pile, the contents of her greenhouse scattered every which way.

Because the man couldn't walk on his own, she'd assisted him to the house in order to bandage him up, only to discover he was messed up eight ways from Sunday. Now he had the nerve to tell her he couldn't remember who the heck he was, let alone what he was doing dumped pretty much at the side of the highway in the middle of the night.

Daisy picked up the phone and started dialing. She needed a friend. She needed somebody strong enough to do some heavy lifting if necessary, somebody loyal enough to come to her aid at a moment's notice without putting up too much of a fuss. It wasn't everyday that a woman found an injured man in her rose garden. Above all, she felt excited.

Getting the stranger medical care presented a real problem, especially since the man didn't remember his own name. Was he lying to get sympathy? Daisy wondered. Or was he telling the truth?

Two

Chester Whitcomb arrived in fifteen minutes. Dark brown, of good build and great looks, Chester had been a reliable friend and able-bodied employee of Daisy's for two years.

Until this early morning wake-up and rescue call from Daisy, Chester had been no trouble at all. But this morning, instead of being a help, Chester had set himself in direct opposition to Daisy's wants and the stranger's needs.

He had taken one look at the scruffy stranger, kicked back at Daisy's kitchen table, an ice pack on his banged-up face, and said in a don't-mess-with-me tone, "Daisy, I don't like this at all. He doesn't belong here."

Chester's open animosity created tension for all involved. Daisy didn't care; she was determined to help the injured man. She was also determined Chester would help her do it. "Thanks for coming so fast. Let's haul him to my truck."

Chester folded his arms against his chest. He didn't look like he was even close to budging from where he stood in the kitchen, directly across the table from the injured man. He nearly snarled his next words. "Call the police."

"No."

"Then I'll do it." He shoved Daisy aside.

She stepped up to him, her voice set on smooth. "No, Chester. I called you over here to help me get him to the hospital. I don't need to be rescued." She pointed at her guest. "This guy does. We're gonna help him."

Chester was a study in disgust. His body was a long stiff line of negative energy. His top lip had a slight curl to it. "This guy claims he doesn't know his own name. That's a police problem, Daisy."

"Let the doctor call in the police, if necessary. Right now, the man needs our help, Chester. Either do what I want you to do or go home."

Chester gave Daisy a once-over. She had removed her red bandanna to reveal hair swept off her face and controlled with two leopard-print Goody brand barrettes. In place of the green garden clogs were white deck shoes. She still wore sweats.

In Chester's mind, she looked young and vulnerable. She looked as if she was having a ball. Thoroughly disgruntled, he said, "I'm not leaving you alone with him." He said the word *him* like a curse.

Daisy shoved her hands on her hips. "I was alone with him before you got here, wasn't I? Nothing happened."

"It could have," Chester argued.

"But it didn't. Let's stop wasting time."

"I don't like this, Daisy."

"Neither do I, but the man needs help. He showed up in my yard and I'm gonna help him. You do whatever you wanna do. Just stay out of my way."

Chester bit off a curse. "Damn, you're stubborn."

"Thank you."

"You're not welcome."

The two men glared at each other. They were both in

the six-foot range. They were both well built. It was obvious that neither man trusted the other. They were tense. Their jaws were clamped shut. Their hands were rolled into fists.

Cutie Pie looked from one male to the other. She barked once as if to warn them she wouldn't tolerate any fighting in Daisy's kitchen.

Daisy patted her guardian angel on the top of her head. "Atta girl. You keep 'em in line."

To the men she said, "Quit fooling around, boys. Chester, you get him into the truck while I get my purse. I'll be right back." She patted her four-legged friend. "Cutie Pie, you stay here."

Cutie Pie went to a corner where she could watch Daisy come and go and she could also have a full view of the two glaring men. She laid down with her hind legs coiled beneath her. She'd be ready to leap at either man in an instant.

Both men had eyes only for each other.

Chester approached the stranger as if he wanted nothing more than a single opportunity to chuck the injured man in the trash can and kick that trash can down the street. "I'm not standing you on your feet."

The stranger narrowed his one good eye. "I don't want your help."

"I'm not helping you. I'm helping Daisy."

The stranger got to his feet, lurched toward the table, righted himself, took one step forward, and would have fallen on his face if Chester hadn't grabbed him with both hands. The stranger jerked as if burned.

Chester gripped him hard. "You better not be faking. If I find out you're faking, if I find out you either have or had it in your mind to take advantage of Daisy, I will make it my business to break both your legs."

"Get off me."

Chester tightened his grip before he let the stranger go. "I haven't even got started. Like I said, you better not be faking."

The stranger braced both legs. He teetered a little. To his surprise, it was Cutie Pie who came to stand by his side. Her ears rotated. Her gaze was steady.

Chester wore a stunned expression. "Correction. I'll break both your legs and your arms, too."

The stranger cut him an ugly look. "Over my dead body."

"Don't tempt me."

Daisy entered the room, assessed the drama correctly, and pointed a finger at one, then the other glaring man. "Come on, boys, let's play nice."

Chester shoved his shoulder beneath the stranger's arm. "This isn't a game, Daisy. I hope you know what you're doing."

"If helping someone is wrong, Chester, I don't wanna be right."

"You and your bleeding heart are nothing but trouble. This isn't a lost puppy or a hurt deer on the run. This guy could be and probably is all kinds of bad news."

Daisy was already snapping off lights. "Our job is to get him to the hospital. We'll deal with the rest of what happens whenever it happens."

Chester pushed the stranger through the kitchen door.

The man stepped on Chester's foot.

Daisy took the time to smack both men on the arm. "I said, play nice."

It was a five-mile ride to Logan Hospital and Medical

Center. As Daisy suspected, the emergency room was quiet. The trio walked in without mishap. Within minutes, the stranger was seated on an examination table. But all was not well.

After detailed questioning by the medical team, after X rays were taken, after the X rays were examined, it was determined that the stranger had been badly beaten but was fortunate not to have any broken or cracked bones.

The more serious issue was the stranger's mild concussion. All the hard knocks to his head had left internal and external marks. The stranger was black and blue.

The doctor was a very thin black woman named Martha Randal. She was in her fifties, fit, and very much interested in the patient. "You can't remember a thing about what happened to you?" she asked.

"No."

"Interesting."

The stranger buttoned his own shirt. "I'd like to leave."

The doctor knew it was none of her business, but it had been a long night with too few patients. Besides, she knew Daisy and was concerned about her getting into trouble because she had a heart too full of love.

Dr. Randal inspected her patient one last time even as she reminded herself once again that she ought to be objective. By law, she was required to be objective. But this was Daisy. Everybody in Guthrie had a soft spot for Daisy Rogers.

She was one of those few people in the world who could turn a bad day into something good with a smile and a few kind words. The trouble was, Daisy wasn't hauling a stray pup to the vet. She had herself a man this time. A big one.

The man had no insurance, nor any legal papers. There were no drugs in his system. His body was incredibly fit. His hair was precision cut. He wore no wedding ring, nor any other jewelry. He had no tattoos. No birthmarks.

His teeth were strong. Even his nails were clipped. This was no average homeless man or drug addict. He was a well-spoken man with a strong vocabulary. He had manners. He had amnesia. "Where will you go?"

Daisy interrupted. "Home with me, doctor."

Small, inquisitive eyes scanned the younger woman. The doctor turned her intuitive gaze to the younger woman's friend. She registered that the "friend" was holding his breath like a frustrated child filled with rage.

Had the moment not been so serious, she might have laughed at Daisy's predicament at being forced to choose between aiding an injured man and fending off a mad one. "Do you think this is wise?"

Daisy didn't hesitate. "Under the circumstances, yes."

"Brave woman." The doctor turned brisk. "Of course, I'll be filing a report with the police."

Daisy slung her purse over her shoulder. It was tan leather, heavy, and filled with enough junk to be a lethal weapon. She had thought about using her purse on Chester during their trek from the truck to the emergency room after he'd practically shoved their charge through the emergency-room door.

"Good," she said, her tone decisive. "That way we can find out what happened to him. In the meantime, we'll call him John Doe."

She paid the hospital bill with her Visa credit card, which really ticked Chester off. He looked ready to toss

John Doe on Highway 33, somewhere between Academy Road and Noble Avenue.

"Daisy," he said, "You've gone too far this time."

She smacked his right arm, just above the elbow. "You don't say that when I take an animal I find to get shots at the vet. I always use my Visa for stuff like this. It's how I keep track."

Chester spoke low and to the point. "This guy may be an animal. He might even be a real dog. But he walks on two legs, Daisy. I don't trust a two-legged anything who shows up out of nowhere looking for a handout."

John Doe looked as if he wanted to rip Chester in half with his bare teeth. "I will pay her back." He pronounced each word distinctly.

"How?"

"I don't know. I just will."

Chester hustled John Doe to his truck; he had refused to take Daisy's truck, even though she had insisted. "Get in the back."

John Doe resisted. "No, I'm riding in the cab this time." They both knew that Chester had made him ride in the back so every pain would be magnified. If John Doe was faking his amnesia, Chester was ready with the payback for lying.

He hit every bump he could find down Highway 33 to Logan Hospital. There were loose tools, trash, cans, and a spare wheel in the bed of Chester's truck. He wanted to make sure John Doe didn't forget he wasn't welcome.

Chester glared at John Doe, who glared right back. Neither man moved. Without breaking their glare, both men said at the same time, "Daisy?"

"Of course, gentlemen. I'll be glad to sit in the middle."

Briefly, Daisy wondered at the wisdom of climbing between a raging bull and an injured bull. Her daddy had taught her how to fight, how to be strong, and when to do the right thing, which is why she found herself in her present predicament: coming to the aid of an injured stranger.

Her mom had taught her to listen to her heart. Her heart said, "Give the stranger a chance." And so she did.

From the sliding doors at the emergency-room entrance, Dr. Randal watched the mismatched trio. She planned to call the police right away. But first, she wanted to call Daisy's mother.

Four miles from home, the Nokia cell phone in Daisy's purse rang. It was a show tune melody. "Hello?"

"Girl, are you crazy?"

"No, Mom."

"If Martha hadn't called me, I just don't know what I would have done."

Daisy was tempted to say that if Martha hadn't called, her mother would still be in bed asleep and minding her own business instead of her daughter's. What Daisy said instead was, "Mom, everything is gonna be fine. Chester is here."

Chester turned a wicked glare at John Doe. His fingers flexed against the steering wheel of his dark red Dodge Ram. "Yeah. Chester is here."

John Doe responded with a curl of his cut upper lip. It was a gruesome sight. Neither man gave Daisy a lick of attention.

She held up the peace sign and aimed it at each man. She wished she had Cutie Pie on hand to help referee. Open animosity from the two men created tension for all

involved. She broke the tense situation into one manage-
able bit at a time.

The first bit was to deal with her cell-phone call. "No,
Mom, don't come over."

After a pause she added, "No, Mom, I'm not mad at
Dr. Randal. She's your best friend and this is a small town.
She let loyalty get in the way of good judgment. It should
have been the police she called, not my mother."

John Doe tensed beside Daisy. She patted him on the
leg before explaining to her mother. "Not that I think John
Doe's gonna be any trouble."

"John Doe?" her mother asked.

Exasperated that she had to deal with explanations before she got her guest settled in at the house, Daisy rolled
her eyes before explaining. "That's what I'm calling him
until all this amnesia business is straightened out."

"Girl, if your father was alive, he'd . . . he'd . . ."

"Be here instead of Chester." There was no mistaking
Daisy's love for her mother. It was there in the softening
of her tone. But she took full responsibility for her current
rescue mission. "Go back to bed, Mom. I'll call you before
lunch."

"What about the shop?"

"The shop will be fine. Don't forget, Chester is here."

Chester's grin was everything nasty. He cut his dark,
belligerent eyes over at John Doe, a man who looked as
if he'd lost a fight with the devil himself. "Yeah. Don't
forget. Chester is here. Chester the leg breaker."

Daisy punched him on the thigh. "Knock it off." She
paused. "No, not you, Mom. Don't worry. I'll call you in
no time. Yes, Mom, if things get hairy at the shop, I'll
give you a buzz."

Three

Things got hairy.

Daisy insisted John Doe stay with her and not with Chester. Her insistence made Chester mad. His anger made him a foe instead of an ally. It was an unpleasant scenario for all three of them.

Daisy stood firm on her decision. "Chester, if you think Cutie Pie is a problem, just wait 'til I call Mom."

He was clearly appalled at the thought. Amanda Rogers was the kind of woman who believed age gave her privilege. She wouldn't think twice about taking a switch to Chester's butt. "Don't do that," he said.

Daisy laughed. "Then behave yourself."

Chester didn't just button his lip. He bit it.

John Doe gave him a look that asked, *Are you a mouse or a man?*

Daisy tossed her leather purse on the kitchen table. "Look, it's Friday morning. While I'm out taking care of business today, I want you to relax, John Doe. Chester, you can either go or stay for now. If you stay, you can help me. If you go, you can call me. I just don't have time to keep the peace. You two need to get along. That's an order."

John Doe studied her without expression. "I don't take orders."

"You don't know what you take," she countered, her head cocked to one side. "You've got amnesia, remember?"

Chester proved he couldn't be counted on to keep his cool. "Yeah, John Doe. You've got amnesia. If I find out you don't have amnesia, I will break your legs, your arms, and your face, too."

Daisy rolled her eyes and put her hands on her hips. It was a classic image of a woman on fire. "I've had enough. My greenhouse is laying in the compost pile. Chester, if you stay, you can pick it up. You know where it goes."

"And while I'm at it, I'll look for his wallet. We need the police out here, Daisy. This guy probably stole a car and stashed it on your property. He's probably got a warrant out for his arrest somewhere."

"I don't believe that, Chester."

Chester's eyes were slits of suppressed rage. "How can you know what to believe, Daisy, when you've never seen this guy before in your life?"

"I've got a gut feeling that I'm doing the right thing here. I'm asking you to be my friend, Chester. That's it."

"I am your friend. That's why I'm so concerned, Daisy." Chester moved around the kitchen making coffee. He knew precisely where the filters were, the coffee grounds, the mugs and all.

Daisy recognized exactly what Chester was doing. He wanted John Doe to understand that only one of them had a good reason to be in her kitchen. That one reason was based on friendship.

When he set two mugs on the table, she put a halt to

his childish power play. "I'm glad you're making coffee. It'll give you guys a chance to get better acquainted. Fellas, I'm going to work."

She scribbled the number to the garden shop on the back of an envelope. She posted the envelope to the front of the refrigerator with a cabbage-shaped magnet. "If you need me, John Doe, call me. I don't plan to baby-sit, and I won't be back until five. Fend for yourself while I'm gone."

She turned to Chester. "If I come back to find holes in my walls or holes in my guest because the two of you have been fighting, you're both gonna catch hell." She pointed at the two mugs on the table. "The rest is on you. I've got twenty minutes to change and get to the shop. If I was you two, I'd behave."

In her bedroom, Daisy ran about the business of getting dressed for work with her hands on automatic. The main thing on her mind was John Doe. Even though she was being upbeat about her situation, she wasn't an airhead and she really wasn't a bleeding heart. She had a level head and a kind personality. She wasn't stupid.

She set her mind to thinking about Chester's number-one worry: whether or not John Doe was a fugitive from the law. She had no history with him so he could easily pretend to have lost his memory and she would never know the difference.

But even if he had lost his memory, some things didn't lie. The way he dressed and the way he spoke were two important clues about his personality: He cared about himself and was educated. This was no thug.

Maybe he had been carjacked and dumped by the side of the road and crawled into her yard. He wasn't all that far from the back door. It was dark. He wouldn't know where he was going with one eye swollen shut and the other squinted up with pain.

He was bruised everywhere, she could see with her eyes, and yet he never once complained. He groaned now and then but that was an involuntary response to excruciating pain. She had to hand it to him for not being a whiner.

Chester was the one getting on her nerves. She wasn't a child and he wasn't her daddy. She could do whatever she wanted to do, and that's exactly why she had no qualms about taking John Doe into her house. People knew he was there. The doctor. Her mother. Chester. And probably the police.

For some reason she couldn't explain, Daisy wanted to keep the police out of the investigation for a while, just long enough for John Doe to get a grip on his own reality or at least get some sleep.

Maybe after some rest in a nonthreatening environment he would be able to sort out his mind and figure out what happened to him within the last twenty-four hours. The doctor had said that his bruises were fresh.

Daisy had noted for herself that he didn't smell rank. Except for the grime from the compost pile and some dried blood, he was otherwise clean. That said a lot. It said that when he'd gotten dressed the morning before, he'd dressed for one day.

That meant he had someplace to lay his hat every night. Homeless people in her experience had layers of clothes and those layers were often dirty or torn. In all cases, the clothes were well worn. This guy's shoes were a name brand and expensive. His running suit was expensive.

In fact, the clothes he wore were dark and athletic, something a guy would wear when he needed maximum mobility and maximum comfort.

Crazy as it was, she took all those objective facts about his personality and used them to form a quick judgment. Quick judgments had everything to do with the unconscious registering of details about personality. She felt good. Whatever happened, she knew it was meant to be.

During her shower, she allowed herself a moment to consider the dark side of her situation. The man could be more than a thug. He could be a killer on the run. The idea of it, the potential for truth in it, made Daisy's skin pebble with goose bumps of misgiving.

Until now, she had appeared strong and fearless in front of John Doe and Chester and the hospital personnel, especially Dr. Randal. But in the quiet privacy of her bedroom, her strength was raw and vulnerable to doubt.

Had John Doe seen her somewhere in town, followed her to her home without her knowing it, thought she was lonely because she was unmarried and lived alone, then set out to manipulate her in order to suit his own devious needs?

Daisy was driving herself crazy thinking about it all. She dressed quickly in jeans, a white T-shirt, and Skechers. She popped the lid of her laundry hamper and dumped the deck shoes inside with the sweats she had worn to rescue John Doe.

The shoes, like the clothes, were smudged, darkened, and dotted with dirt. She couldn't help but wonder if she would become smudged, darkened, and dirty if she developed a relationship with the stranger.

She was running on instinct, but so was Chester. He

wanted to keep her safe. It didn't take a whole lot to figure that he wanted to keep her for himself, that maybe his hostile attitude toward the stranger was purely territorial.

She didn't know for sure because she couldn't read Chester's mind. How could she read his mind when he clearly wasn't thinking straight? She'd watched him shove John Doe and threaten him more than once. His behavior was absurd, totally out of the norm for the boundaries of their relationship.

She did know that he cared about her, that whatever he did was based on that simple fact. She owed it to their relationship to at least think about his cautioning behavior. Her main trouble with Chester was that he was downright antagonistic. She didn't need that kind of drama in an already dramatic situation.

Chester was a problem she couldn't ignore. If he kept pushing John Doe there was bound to be a scuffle. The stranger didn't look or behave like the type of guy who would take any guff from anybody, male or female.

What in John Doe's personality or situation had made him a victim? Had he been in the wrong place at the wrong time, or was he beaten up and dumped unconscious because he was really up to no good and had paid a terrible price for his dirty deeds?

Daisy had nothing but questions, questions she knew Chester was seeking answers to in his angry, combative way. He was there as her friend. He was staying because he felt it was the right thing for a caring friend to do.

Well, she figured, that wasn't exactly true. She couldn't forget he was being territorial. She hadn't realized how territorial he was until now. Their relationship had never been put to any sort of emotional strain or test before.

For the first time, she was seeing Chester in a different light. He wasn't the harmless, caring, platonic friend she took for granted. He was a red-blooded male staking claim with an unknown and powerful male.

She walked straight through the kitchen to the kitchen counter. Both men were sitting at the table, coffee in hand. She poured herself a commuter mug of coffee, put the lid in place, and turned to walk out the door without saying a word.

Enough had been said. She had a business to run and all the players involved were grown-ups, whether they be crooks or good guys. The cards were on the table; whatever happened happened.

She had her hand on the brass doorknob when John Doe croaked, "Wait." She half turned.

Chester sat up straighter in his seat.

John Doe tipped his head. He stared at her with his one good eye. "You're a good woman, Daisy Rogers. I owe you."

She felt lighter than air. It was ridiculous to feel that way when she had known the man less than five hours. The man's injuries were an ugly sight to behold. His eye looked horrible. His lips looked horrible. But like a prize fighter, underneath the black-and-blue was a fine-looking, incredibly well-built man.

She felt a little thrill in her veins.

She tipped her head in return, flashed a jaunty smile, and opened the back door. On the way out, she heard a growl. She wasn't sure if the growl came from Cutie Pie in the corner of the kitchen or from Chester Whitcomb.

If people thought she was a bleeding heart, Daisy mused, so what?

At least her heart bled for a good cause, and the cause was the pursuit of good works in the form of good deeds. Perhaps her attitude was trite, but it was real and it was a natural part of what made her tick.

An innate sense of morality, of right versus wrong, made it possible for her to ignore the discipline of law and do her own thing. She needed answers to serious questions and couldn't afford to wait for Chester to work with the Guthrie police in a painstaking reconstruction of the details leading to John Doe's arrival in her compost pile before she made a decision to help him—or not.

There was only one source to all the true answers: John Doe. By accepting him into her life, however temporarily, she had entered into a contract with him to take his word and his actions at face value.

She was not being naïve; she was being practical. If she doubted everything he said and every move he made, then they would never get anywhere when it came to discovering his true identity. That kind of attitude opposed her Good Samaritan value system.

She had promised John Doe a safe haven to recuperate. She would not betray that initial act of trust. Actually, when she really thought about it, he was in the most vulnerable position of all; he was a stranger in a strange place with no identity—if what he said was true.

She knew she'd told the men she wouldn't baby-sit, but a few minutes later, a vision of Cutie Pie playing referee after all made her pick up the telephone in the shop to call the house. The phone was picked up on the fourth ring.

"John Doe here."

His voice was every bit as deep and delectable as she

remembered, every bit as distracting, but she vowed to stay on task. "It's Daisy."

"There aren't any holes in the walls or broken furniture."

She laughed. "It's good to know you two are behaving yourselves."

"Your friend is gone."

"Really?"

"Yeah. He left right after we checked the compost pile. Sorry about your greenhouse."

"People are more important than things are. Besides, it wasn't broken."

"No, but the stuff you had inside was totally out of order. I didn't know how to fix it but I put everything back on the shelves in a rough sort based on item, size, and similarity."

She was pleased. "Seeds with seeds. Jars with jars?"

"Right."

"Good."

He was endearing himself to her already. A real user and loser would be laid up on the couch with the remote control in his hand if he couldn't sleep, she figured.

This guy was banged up worse than any man or animal she had ever encountered before in her life and yet he made time to do a preliminary investigation into the compost pile and to right the property of hers that he had knocked down.

She liked that attitude.

To keep herself focused on the fact she didn't know him from Jack the Ripper, she aligned the two-cup-sized hand-painted clay pots on the shelf above the telephone according to size. Like her life at the moment, the decorative clay pots were slightly skewed. "Hey, get some rest."

John Doe put down the envelope and pen he had been scratching notes on at the kitchen table when the telephone rang. "I wish I could."

"Somebody is looking for you, John."

"You sound so positive."

"I am."

"Why?"

"A man like you gets noticed." As soon as the words were out, Daisy wanted to bite her tongue. Her words betrayed her attraction.

"And what kind of man is that?"

"Strong. Careful. Observant. Big. Handsome."

His laugh sounded painful. She figured it probably was painful since his ribs were banged up.

"You make me feel good, Daisy. In spite of everything that's wrong in my life right now, I'll never be sorry that I met you. You're one of those rare people who sees the good in people first instead of the bad, and you do it without expecting anything in return. You've got honor, Daisy. I like that in a woman."

"If this situation were normal, we wouldn't talk so freely with each other, but this isn't a normal situation. You don't have a memory. In a way, not having a memory makes you like a child."

"I'm hurt, Daisy, not harmless."

"Nobody who walks on two feet is harmless, even children. You've seen the news. Kids kill kids and their parents, too. I don't think you're harmless, John Doe. I don't even think you're confused. I just think you're in a tough situation right now. I think that mainly you need a friend."

"We haven't known each other long enough to be friends," John Doe argued. "I can see why Chester is so bent out of shape. At first I thought it was because he was jealous of your attention to me but now I see that if I were him, I'd be bent out of shape."

"What do you mean?"

He explained. "You're way too trusting, Daisy. I know you're safe from me, but you don't know you're safe from me. I'm an acquaintance and not even one with a good reputation. I have no reputation at all."

"Since I've seen you in your underwear at the hospital I can't say we're exactly acquaintances. The fact is, John Doe, you need somebody to lean on until you can stand on your own feet without being ready to fall down. You're no longer a victim. You're a survivor. We have a bond based on that transition. It's kind of like helping a lady have a baby in an elevator. The relationship is an intimate one even though the players are strangers. It's a bond that can't be broken."

"You're incredible."

"And you have to be ready to fall flat on the floor. Even if you can't sleep, at least lie down. If you aren't thinking so hard about figuring out who you are, maybe you'll remember something important, and I'm not just talking about your name, either."

"How I got here is driving me crazy. There is no car. I have no keys. No wallet. No identification. Not even jewelry. But I'm alive. Simple logic says I ought to have been found dead at the side of the road and not dumped in somebody's yard."

"I figured that, too. Someone out there knows exactly who you are and how you got here."

"That's why I can't rest," John Doe admitted. "Your life is in danger."

"Could be in danger. But whose life isn't in danger? Let's face it, I don't live all that far from an airport. A plane could drop on top of the house and I'd be dead and French-fried. I have a business that caters to the public. Somebody could drop a smoldering cigarette on a dry windy day and that cigarette could cause a fire while I'm asleep at night. Again, I could be dead and French-fried. Danger is all over the place."

"Danger doesn't always land in the compost pile."

"See, you've got a sense of humor, too. Like I said, somebody somewhere knows you're missing. A guy like you would get noticed."

"You're implying that I have a woman in my life."

"Most good men do."

"Which brings me back to the point I was making about danger. One thing I do know, I am a danger to you. Someone beat me into a near coma but chose to let me live. They couldn't know I'd have amnesia. They'll be wondering why I didn't turn up again wherever it is I belong. The fact that whoever beat me up will come back is why my being here puts you in danger."

Daisy was all business. "Then *danger* is your middle name, and I'm still not changing my mind about you."

"Chester was right about one thing."

"What?"

"We should involve the police."

"Because we're dealing with a *they* kind of danger and not a *who* kind of danger?"

"Exactly. I didn't walk over to the compost pile. I was unconscious. I'm too big to be carried. It's possible but not likely. I don't have any bruises on my body that co-incide with being hefted by another man."

"That means at least two people are involved."

"You'd make a great detective."

"I do like mystery novels. Hey, wouldn't it be a hoot if you turned out to be a real PI?" She said this with wonder and relish.

"Yeah. A real hoot."

Daisy smiled even though he couldn't see it. Chester might think John Doe was a fake, but something told her to give him the benefit of the doubt in the form of open hospitality. Right now, because Chester resisted her deci-sion to allow the stranger refuge on her property until his identity crisis was resolved, he had also set himself up to play the enemy in the minor drama of her life.

Until now, his friendship and loyalty had never been a package deal she questioned. Until now, he had always been a friend she counted on without question.

Until now, he had been someone she trusted completely.

Why hadn't he given John Doe the benefit of the doubt as she had? Was it simple male jealousy Chester felt when he saw John Doe? Or was Chester's problem deeper than machismo?

She hoped to find out.

Four

Despite a night of broken sleep and the shock of finding John Doe knocked out in her garden, for Daisy, the day was perfect. No matter how rocky the night, going to work at her business made her world right again.

Her gardening business was more than a hobby; it was her life's work. Making a living doing the work she loved, right on her own property, formed the center of her personal power. As it was her custom to open Daisy's Rose and Garden Shop alone, she had no time to waste.

She had to remove the chairs from the tops of the two round courtesy tables, make coffee, and be sure the cream, sugars, and stirrers were stocked on the customer convenience counter before the first customers arrived.

A heavy coffee drinker herself, Daisy had quickly discovered many of her customers enjoyed a cup while browsing her public garden. The scent of coffee brewing created a restful, friendly atmosphere. The more time customers spent browsing the aisles and shelves, the more money they tended to spend in the garden shop.

Daisy was pleasantly surprised when the first person through the door was John Doe. She had expected him to feel too bruised and sore to be of much assistance to himself, let alone to her. She admired the inner strength of will which drove him to keep moving even when he had to be at his physical limits.

She punched the On switch for the industrial-sized coffee machine and smiled. "To what do I owe the pleasure?"

Smiling back, John Doe walked over to the customer convenience counter. His stride was stiff, his face a sight, but his spirits were up. "I just thought I'd stop by, make sure you don't need any help after all the . . . commotion." His voice was a little too casual for the way his eyes darted about the gardening room. "By the way, where's Chester?"

Daisy grabbed a Tupperware container marked ICED COFFEE, then filled it with cubes from the small stainless-steel ice machine. She served coffee two ways: hot and cold. No decaf. No tea. Just strong black brew.

She felt that most problems were easier to face after a cup of coffee. "Running late, I guess. Haven't heard from him, but he'll be here. He said he'll bring you a change of clothes."

John Doe grabbed a mug from the counter. The mug was embossed with the Daisy's Rose and Garden Shop logo, a set of three pink and peach cabbage roses tied with flowing purple ribbon.

The company logo was set in a cream square against a forest green background, a color scheme repeated throughout the garden shop. John Doe thought the business had the feel of a cozy conservatory or sunroom addition to a private home.

He had to remind himself this was a place of business.

"I apologize again for throwing you off your schedule," he said, not yet relaxed enough to let his guard down to sleep as she had suggested he do until his strength returned.

"Hey, you!" Daisy smiled at him. "Don't you know that good rest and good food are the cure-alls for most ailments? You should be resting that beat-up body of yours."

"I was sitting down in the living room when I realized I hadn't heard Chester pull up. Is his being late going to cause a problem for you?" John Doe asked.

"He'll be here."

"I noticed a delivery truck a little while ago and figured he'd show up soon to put your things away. When he didn't come along, I came over."

John Doe's look was cool, almost arrogant as he studied Daisy. She figured it was pride stamped on his injured face. Along with his battered body, she suspected there was also the issue of his ego.

She had the idea John Doe wasn't accustomed to a woman taking care of him. She hadn't thought of his rescue from his perspective until now. When she did, she realized that it was more than willpower that kept him on his feet—it was pride. "That was nice of you," she said, "but everything is fine. And you're very observant about Chester. Normally he would have been here to meet the delivery man for such a large shipment. But as you know, things aren't exactly business as usual around here right now. Still, don't worry."

His stance relaxed as he continued to look around him. "By the size of the coffeemaker and the number of cups you have on the counter, I figure you either have a lot of customers who drink coffee or you drink a lot of coffee yourself. If you're expecting a rush, I'd be glad to do what I can."

Daisy added several bags of potato chips to a round wicker basket, then set the basket next to a huge jar of chocolate-dipped biscotti. "Tonight I'm hosting a meeting. It'll be busier then. Besides, the doors aren't open officially yet. I'm just setting things up now." She winked at him.

She added, "I've got a feeling it's gonna be hectic around here after tonight. Once news travels about who you are and how you came to be at my place, the nosy folks will come around and boost sales. Don't worry. Things are fine. Actually, I think you really ought to be lying down. You look awful."

"I agree, but I wanted to be sure you're okay before I take time out. Once I crash, I'll be out for a while. It's probably best your customers don't see me, anyway. At least not today. I'll just grab some coffee, if it's all right with you, and then head back to the house before you officially open for business."

Daisy looked him up and down. She had to hand it to him for his positive attitude. If his purpose in seeking her out was to make sure she understood he had no intention of being a freeloader, then his mission had been accomplished. "It's all right with me." She pointed a thumb in the direction of the coffeemaker. "Knock yourself out." She grinned wide. "Pun intended."

John Doe helped himself to coffee. He liked it strong. He liked it black. As Daisy wandered about the shop watering plants, he took a moment to consider what bothered him the most about the scenario he shared with Daisy:

Chester. Chester was the reason he couldn't sleep, even though he was exhausted enough to fall on his face.

Something about Chester's absence made him wary. Chester knew Daisy had a strange man in her house, knew she had to be stressed, claimed to be a great friend, and yet he was nowhere in sight.

Maybe he had a good explanation for not being there, but whatever it was, John Doe doubted his reason would be enough to satisfy him.

Daisy shouldn't have been left alone no matter how self-sufficient she appeared to be. Unless she was packing a concealed weapon and had the nerve to use it to kill, she was in a vulnerable position.

John Doe respected Chester for coming quickly to Daisy's aid initially, but he didn't respect him for taking off. Maybe Chester had been late for a shipment delivery before and Daisy wasn't worried.

But his absence just didn't feel right to John Doe, especially after Chester had made such a fuss about Daisy taking him home in the first place. His absence now didn't jibe with his prior actions.

"You've got five minutes before I open the doors," Daisy said. She slipped a Miles Davis cassette into the stereo system. The haunted sound of his wailing horn fit her mood perfectly.

She felt something wail inside her because she had the feeling John Doe's arrival had changed her life in some significant way. She just didn't know how. Was it his quiet strength despite having had the crap beat out of him? Or was it the easy way she felt about him despite the fact he didn't know his own name?

John Doe rinsed his mug. "Even though I drank this

coffee I'm pretty much spent. The caffeine gives me just enough energy to get from the garden shop to the house. I won't be much good to you or me if I don't get some rest."

His pause was thoughtful, his expression unreadable. "Let me know if you need me, Daisy. I might shock a few customers with my appearance, but you don't have to lift or haul anything heavy. I'll do it."

Suddenly, his concern for her made Daisy feel shy, feminine, and special. She busied herself by picking yellow leaves off the lavender-flowered cyclamen. Inside the garden shop, she had a small section of flowering houseplants. "Thanks."

Their eyes caught and held.

It was then that Chester walked in. "Tell me if I've got this straight," he said, his voice soft and way too calm to Daisy's ears. "You met this guy out of the blue and now you two are all chatty. This isn't gonna work."

Daisy stepped up to him. "Don't. Start."

She stalked off to stand behind the cash register. Chester rarely got on her nerves, but his attitude really made her angry. She believed in fair play, which meant giving John Doe a fair shake. Besides, she thought spitefully, John Doe was right, Chester should have been there to meet the delivery man.

Chester threw an old, crumpled, blue plastic Wal-Mart shopping bag at John Doe. "Here's some clothes." They were old, too.

Daisy looked away from Chester and counted to ten before she smacked him. As she counted, she looked through the glass front of the garden shop at the parking lot. The lot was covered in gray pea gravel and was empty of cars. She didn't expect the lot to stay empty much longer.

Soon the early-bird customers would arrive and there would be no time for small talk. She had to get this potentially volatile situation between the two iron-headed men under control. John Doe was as stubborn as Chester.

Daisy sighed in dismay. No one would get any peace if the men didn't get along. "At ease, gentlemen."

To Chester she said, "John Doe was just leaving."

Chester's nostrils were flared. He spoke to Daisy but his eyes were on John Doe. "You can always count on me." He paused for emphasis. "Any day. Any time."

Daisy shook her head a little, amazed at how quickly the threat of her personal danger could instill some ancient male code of honor between two totally different men. She could understand why Chester would want to protect her from John Doe.

She couldn't understand why John Doe would want to protect her from Chester. She waved Chester off with a nervous laugh. "This is nuts. Haven't you two heard the saying, 'Go with the flow'?"

When neither man answered, she said, "Start flowing. John Doe, it's early, go to bed. Chester, help Mr. Dillingsworth down from his truck. He only drives that thing when he means business. Last time he drove his old diesel he bought fourteen roses, ten companion plants and five bags of shredded cypress to use as mulch in his garden."

John Doe looked into Daisy's pretty face and wondered again how she managed to remain unattached. He wasn't surprised Chester was so rude and possessive. He was surprised that Daisy showed a complete lack of sexual interest in Chester. She treated him like a brother. It had to drive Chester crazy.

Daisy felt tension sizzle and pop in the air. At the moment, she could do without the company of either man. They had messed up her quiet early-morning euphoria. "Come on, you two. Move it."

The men moved, both of them stiff. John Doe was stiff because he'd been worked over by professional thugs. Chester was stiff because she was ordering him around and he clearly didn't like it.

Daisy tamped down on her anger. She had a right to do whatever she wanted to do with whomever she wanted. She was over twenty-one. Chester needed to mind more of his own personal business and less of hers.

John Doe needed to find the rest of his own mind so he could get back home where he belonged. She needed to get back into her comfort zone. Daisy grabbed her company mug and threw back the last of her coffee, lukewarm now but still tasty. God, she loved coffee!

Mr. Dillingsworth pushed Chester aside so he could walk through the door of Daisy's Rose and Garden Shop first. "I hear you've got some new miniroses!" he hollered.

"I do."

"Well, show 'em to me quick before Zenith gets here!" the seventy-year-old gardener ordered. Mr. Dillingsworth was hard of hearing and shouted his conversation at every occasion. "I want her to wonder what she missed!"

His eyes flashed with devilment. They both knew he and Zenith had a rivalry that never let up. There were forty years between them in age, but they got along with each other as if they'd grown up on the same playground.

Mr. Dillingsworth lifted his nose in the air to smell the

coffee, a vice he'd learned to do without because it raised his blood pressure too high. "Buying up the miniroses is my favorite way to get Zenith over to see the changes in my garden. You know how she is when it comes to getting first dibs on your new shipments. I might buy the whole lot just to drive that gal up the wall."

Daisy had a duplicate shipment of miniroses due the following week. Zenith would make sure she was in to get what she missed this time around. Happy to benefit from her customers' friendly rivalry, Daisy stepped from behind the register, ready to pursue the first sale of the day.

Mr. Dillingsworth extended his left elbow for her to hold onto as a gentlemanly courtesy. With his right hand, he patted the top pocket of his jean coveralls. Daisy knew from experience that inside that pocket was a wad of cash held together with a thick rubberband. Mr. Dillingsworth didn't use a wallet.

Chester went to the convenience counter to pour himself a mug of coffee. As he added cream and sugar, even he had to smile at Mr. Dillingsworth's obvious pleasure at getting one up on his gardening rival, Zenith. He raised his mug in silent salute to the bargaining ritual he knew Daisy enjoyed.

"Aah," Daisy said as she acknowledged his gesture with a wink. "That's better." To Mr. Dillingsworth she said, "Come on, you old troublemaker. Let's give Zenith something to shout about."

While Daisy perused the new shipment of miniroses with her first customer of the day, Chester studied John Doe as he continued his stiff-legged walk to Daisy's house. Chester's expression was easy to read, had anyone been looking.

Five

When Daisy returned home for lunch, John Doe was asleep on the couch. He looked huge. She wasn't surprised he hadn't crashed in the guest bed, although it would have been more fitting for a body his size. Being in bed in the middle of the day probably felt strange to an active man, even one with amnesia. Going to bed in the middle of the day in a strange house, fully dressed as John Doe was, would be even more uncomfortable, she imagined.

She didn't think she could do it either.

As her intriguing guest slept, she looked her fill at the image he presented. He was thick with muscle, strong and hard. He was relaxed on her couch, as if he belonged there, with his shoes off and his long legs covered with the cream knit throw rug she kept on the hearth for such occasions.

The sudden jolt of nerves Daisy felt at seeing him again, even though she expected to see him, caused her fingers to tremble against the mug of coffee she held in her hand. It was her fifth cup of the day.

She would have four more cups before her day at the garden shop was done. Downing excessive amounts of gourmet coffee was her number-one vice, and she thoroughly enjoyed it.

She breathed deep of the steam still rising from the dark brew. As she sipped the rich-tasting blend, she wondered what to do next. It was she who couldn't relax now. She couldn't relax because now she felt aware of John Doe as a woman is aware of a man when she finds him attractive.

At first, he was simply a stray like any other creature she might find in her garden in need of rescue. But in less than one day, after a few well-chosen sentences and a surprise appearance at the garden shop, he had displayed a winning personality, a quality of mind that shined through his bruises and pain.

John Doe had character, and she liked that in a man. Daisy believed strong character was an attribute that didn't wrinkle or sag or fall down with time, it just got better and better. She had the feeling he would make a great friend.

John Doe spoke with his eyes closed. "Sit down, Daisy. I don't bite."

He had sensed her welcome presence, the soft fragrance of her distinctive perfume mixed with the addictive aroma of hot black coffee. Both scents were acquired tastes, and he enjoyed them both.

At the deep, half-asleep sound of his voice, Daisy felt as if her every nerve revved with extra pep. God, he was observant. He reminded her of one of those heroes in Western romance novels, the kind of male hero who senses everything, knows everything without looking or touching. Never had a man shown his awareness of her in such a way.

Daisy was thrilled.

She assessed this moment with John Doe as a woman and not as a Good Samaritan, something that shocked her. This was no ordinary situation, no ordinary man. She could only imagine how awesome John Doe would be when he had his full memory and life restored to him. Who was he? Who?

"Well, I do," she finally said. "Bite that is."

John Doe ignored her flip response to concentrate on her skin. He liked it. As she stood above him, Daisy's skin glowed beneath the soft light of the end table lamps. He had kept them on, as if the child inside him had been afraid.

A part of his mind was gone, possibly never to come back again, yet this woman had given him hope and the space to recover the separate parts of himself in peace. She humbled him with her straightforward manner, her down-home goodness. Perhaps she was a guardian angel, his angel.

Whatever Daisy was, she had given him hope.

"You're one gutsy lady."

He left out how lucky he felt to be resting on her couch in the cool quiet of her home instead of in a homeless shelter of some kind on a loaner cot, but his gratitude was there in the tone of his voice, in his body language.

Gone was the pride he displayed in the garden shop before the arrival of Mr. Dillingsworth early that morning. In the place of pride was the simple truth: he didn't know who he was or how he had arrived in Guthrie.

His mind had shut down, but why? He might never find the answer, never find his way home again. Never. Such a lonely tragic word, he thought grimly, a word he didn't like one bit. He did like Daisy. He used his gaze to tell her so.

The mug of coffee she held wobbled. Daisy recognized a heartfelt compliment when she got one. She set the coffee down on a tall, square end table and was careful to keep the look on her face steady.

His voice had been low, his eyes opened slightly, one eye more open than the other eye because of his recent beating. His lashes, she noticed, were short and thick, some curling at odd angles.

"You feel better," she announced.

"Yes."

"That means you're basically pretty healthy. Had you been in worse physical shape, I don't think you'd recover so quickly."

"I agree." From a sitting position, he looked around her home with a discerning eye. It was clean and well organized, like Daisy. "Nice place."

Her palms sweated, though she kept her expression neutral. "Thanks, and really, I do appreciate you stopping by the shop the way you did this morning."

"When do you rest?"

"All the time. Working with plants is a peaceful business. Plants don't complain. They don't talk back. They don't get into politics. They just look good and keep me busy. The bending and lifting keeps me in shape. My customers are plant people and plant people are usually pretty laid-back anyway. I get to run my mouth about my hobby and nobody gets tired of listening. It's great."

John Doe relaxed his back against the couch. "I'm impressed."

The compliment warmed Daisy, but her stomach was

all butterflies. To soothe her jittery nerves, she reached inside the drawer of the nearest end table, the place where she kept her stash of feel-good food. She tilted the open plastic bag of semisweet chocolate morsels in his direction.

He tossed a chocolate tidbit into his grinning mouth. "You make me laugh inside, Daisy. Chocolate candy is the last thing I'd expect you to pull out of that drawer."

Her nerves were calmed by his charm and humor. There was no negative energy or aggression coming from him, not the way it had come from him inside the garden shop when Chester had arrived late for the morning delivery.

"What did you expect?" she asked. "A gun?"

"I don't know. Just not a yellow bag of Nestlé morsels."

Daisy cleared her throat. No matter how much she rationalized, it still felt weird for her to come home to a man reclining on her couch. Even with the lights on, his clothes on, and their lack of backstory together, John Doe's presence smacked of intimacy. Opening the end table drawer again, she pulled out a rock. She tossed the rock to him.

He caught the stone with ease. "A chunk of amethyst crystal?"

Enjoying a versatile man, she tipped her head in salute. "I see you're more than a handsome face."

"Much more."

She continued. "In ancient Egypt, crystals were used to heal. Many people of that time believed amethyst protected them from snake bites. In Rome, people drank from amethyst goblets in the belief the gem kept them sober."

"Are you trying to heal me with magic, Daisy?"

She eyed him with increasing respect. He wasn't laughing at her. He was listening to her.

"In a way," she replied. "In our time, many people believe amethyst crystals bring creativity and enlightenment to whoever wears them. I don't think you need creativity right now, but you could use some enlightenment."

John Doe noticed she wore a set of multicolored polished stones. "How does someone go about choosing a crystal of any color?"

"It doesn't take special training to choose a rock crystal," Daisy replied. "Your instincts will couple with a stone's positive strength, an energy you'll feel good about when the joining is right."

The words *couple* and *joining* set John Doe's imagination in a lively spin. He wondered if Daisy's life-affirming energy drew him to her the way she drew on the energy generated by polished crystals for healing.

The fact that she was at ease with the ideas she presented him showed John Doe she had a liberal mind. A liberal mind believed in the autonomy of the individual, in free thinking, in pushing the limits of convention and morality.

He admired these qualities in her. "So what you're saying is that crystals make a person's natural energy more strong."

"By George," she teased, "I think you've got it."

She finally sat down.

"Color affects us in many ways," she explained. "Our eyes see color, our mind analyzes it. Our emotions make what our eyes and mind see a personal experience. Take the garden shop. Green is restful. I use white tables as an accent color. The shop is full of windows so there is lots of natural light. Light lifts the spirit. Roses are the universal flower of love. The muted shades of the roses and the variety of house plants give the garden shop a cozy feeling."

His interest in her words was keen. Daisy was more than a pretty face and a giving heart. She was a savvy businesswoman. "You use subliminal messages to make your customers feel welcome."

"Yeah. I use color and texture the way a supermarket uses music and the absence of clocks to encourage shoppers to spend more time in their store. The more time a customer spends browsing a store's merchandise, the more likely the customer is to indulge in impulse buying. Impulse buying adds up quick. I keep inexpensive house plants near the cash register for just that reason."

During her speech, John Doe watched her lips move. They were soft and full. They were dressed in red-brown. He wanted to kiss those lips.

"What does red signify?" he asked, having decided her lipstick color was more red than brown.

"Inner strength. Power."

She crossed the room. From the fireplace mantle, she removed a carved wooden box. Inside the box were polished crystals. She took them out of the small box.

"John Doe, I want you to lie on the white carpet in the center of the room. I'm gonna drag the coffee table out of the way."

The lift of one brow was the only indication he found her request unusual. "Put my shoes on or keep them off?"

Daisy eyed his long, thick legs and big feet. "Whatever works for you."

"I'll keep them off then."

Squashing the urge to laugh at his predicament, John Doe stretched his heavy body full-length over the top of the plush carpet, a huge rectangle centered on a gleaming hardwood floor. "Ready."

"Good," she decided. "We'll begin."

Removing her own shoes, Daisy knelt beside him on the carpet. Systematically, she placed crystals around his body. She explained each crystal's color and purpose as she went along.

At the end of her crystal placement ritual, she spoke with soft authority. "You're lying on a white carpet because white is made of every shade in the color spectrum. White means completion."

John Doe was enthralled. Being with Daisy took his thoughts off his aches and pains. There he was, lying in the middle of her living room floor, surrounded by a variety of colored quartz crystals, all to please a woman who believed in the miracles of human kindness and positive energy.

Right then, he felt blessed to be in her company, spiritually revived. Without really thinking about why, John Doe took her hand in his, raised her hand to his lips, and brushed her glowing skin briefly with a kiss.

She understood the gesture for exactly what it was, a promise of wonderful things to come, in his life and in hers. There was nothing sexual about his touch, only a basic need to connect with another human being.

Above all things, Daisy believed people came into each other's lives for positive reasons. Touching was positive. Goodwill was positive. Companionship was positive. Touching, goodwill, and companionship formed the subtleties of friendship.

When she discovered John Doe abandoned and alone in the compost pile, he had been at rock bottom in his life, so low he physically lay in the dirt, oblivious to his predicament and his surroundings.

She was the hand that literally lifted him from rock bottom into daybreak, a beginning composed of fine possibilities instead of desperate ones. His return to good health had started with a trip to Logan Hospital and Medical Center instead of a trip to the Guthrie police station; one place inspired hope, the other fear. Daisy's act of kindness had been the difference between a stable new start for John Doe and a rocky one.

Because of her helping hand, his efforts to rediscover himself weren't hindered by the pursuit of the essentials of food, clothing, or shelter. In her home, those needs were met. John Doe was able to focus his mental energy on the single-minded construction of a healthy future instead of on merely existing in a troubled present.

His being in her home was not one-sided; he gave her something, too. He gave her an adventure, the mystery of his identity to solve, a treat to look forward to during the breaks of her business day. She never imagined she would be a key player in a mystery.

She whispered, "Yeah. Life is good."

He squeezed her hand in friendship. "Yeah."

At lunch, he presented her with a single lavender rose. "It's from your kitchen garden. I see you have herbs mixed with a few flowers outside the back door."

She traced a nail over the curve of the perfect bud. "Thank you." She placed the rose beside her plate on the dining room table.

"The pleasure"—he bowed slightly from the waist, then winced because his chest hurt—"is all mine."

She felt like one of her Nestlé chocolate morsels: sleek, brown, and scrumptious. To still the butterflies in her stomach, she struck up a neutral conversation. "This combination we had delivered from Pizza Hut is dynamite."

He scooted the box closer to her side of the table. "The way your stomach is growling, I'm glad we ordered extra large."

She sipped lemon-lime soda from a striped plastic straw. "This is wild. We can talk about silly things, a pizza, while all this . . . other stuff is going on at the same time. I can almost forget your real life is a mystery."

John Doe was calm. "I'd never hurt you."

"Not on purpose." Calm as he sounded, Daisy felt his gaze as if he saw straight through her skin, right into her soul.

"No," he said. "Not on purpose."

"At least you're honest."

For a moment, words failed him. He turned his attention to the living room. The main colors in her living room were red and purple. Red leather covered twin couches, and a white area rug lay beneath a green steel-based coffee table designed in a rectangle shape.

On either side of the sofa were purple ceramic lamps on mated square end tables. Gold picture frames and brass ornaments were scattered on the tables. The white rug and vaulted ceiling kept the room from feeling dark.

After a full ten seconds John Doe said, "I would expect a gardener to have a room full of green plants. Enormous ficus or giant elephant ears or something like that."

"Because I work at home, I want the transition from

work to home to be clear. I keep the gardening stuff outside."

"Your living room is a toss-up between a bowl of flowers and a bucket of colored rocks. The idea came to me when I was lying on the floor with all the crystals surrounding me."

She grimaced, but never took her eyes off his rugged face, animated now with a quiet delight. "There aren't any flower patterns in this room."

Again, he scanned the combined living room and dining room, an open floor plan he found appealing. Abstract prints were layered on the walls, and huge amethyst crystals rested on the top shelf of a solid pine curio. A cluster of green metal candleholders with purple, red, and gold candles sat in the center of a six-setting dining room table.

Even the huge matching pine buffet was filled with shining bric-a-brac instead of traditional dishes. Stands of ivy topiary stood on either side of a white painted brick fireplace, the living room's focal point. Her place was grounded, yet full of adventure, like Daisy.

"It's all the color," he decided. "You've got deep red, dark green, dark purple, royal blue, and bright yellow all over the place. The colors are strong, but the throw pillows are soft and cozy-looking. My place is probably chrome and leather."

She watched him meander through her living space. He looked at everything, touching those pieces he found most pleasing. After their pizza lunch, she felt even more relaxed about revealing her private space to him. "My mother says my house is so busy she's never sure whether she should sit down or hunt for bargains."

John Doe's big hands fondled an abalone shell, its center filled with polished crystals. "She's got a point." He replaced the large seashell on the fireplace mantle, only to turn to her instead.

Studying her, John Doe decided she was very much like a curio shop herself, the human embodiment of the bright, the unusual, the one-of-a-kind. Entering her private world provided him with a renewed sense of wonder in living.

He doubted he would be having pizza for lunch if he'd been dumped by the side of the road near someone else's home instead of in Daisy's garden.

Daisy found it tough to focus on anything but the hard body sharing her breathing space. The more time she spent with John Doe, talking with him, observing his habits, the easier it was for her to forget his battered appearance and personal mystery.

John Doe exuded calm and confidence.

"I'd better get back," she said.

"Go ahead. I'll clean up here."

"Okay."

"See you soon."

Still, she lingered. "Soon." Daisy returned to her public garden, to Chester, and looked forward to seeing John Doe again.

Being with him was a little like nibbling a bag of Nestlé chocolate morsels; one bite wasn't enough.

Six

An hour after closing it was time for Daisy to host her monthly garden club meeting. Instead of discussing roses, she bet the topic of discussion would be John Doe. It was bound to be a bawdy discussion.

The women had been friends a good long time, so anything that could be said on the subject, good or bad, would probably be said tonight.

In preparation for the onslaught of questions to come, Daisy wanted to get everything straight in her own mind about what had happened since John Doe's arrival on her property. Of all the things she had put in her compost pile, she never imagined finding a man in there.

She decided to concentrate on what constituted a good compost pile as the focus of her discussion with the garden club. The generic subject tied in well with the more specific subject, John Doe.

Daisy lifted a red pen from the pencil cup near the telephone console. She wrote on a plain piece of printer paper:

WHAT IS COMPOST?

1. A mixture of decaying vegetation and manure
2. Used as a fertilizer and soil conditioner

3. Benefits: slow release of nutrients, improved soil drainage and water retention

COMPOSTING DOS

1. Use pet hair, vegetable-based kitchen scraps, grass clippings, dry leaves, straw, hay
2. Turn the compost pile regularly
3. Keep the pile warm and moist, without being soggy, by putting it in a ventilated spot with great drainage

COMPOSTING DON'TS

1. Skip using pet waste, meat products, or bones, as these will attract unwanted pests such as curious animals and flies
2. Keep weeds out of the pile, even chopped up weeds, because they can regenerate and grow

That done, she turned her thoughts again to John Doe. Systematically, she made a timeline of events since his arrival. She drew a diagonal line across each event, beginning with the sound of the greenhouse falling on top of him and ending with their pizza lunch.

Even though Chester and Dr. Randal thought she was being careless, she wasn't at all. She believed it was possible to be kind and to be careful. To accomplish this, she used clear thinking.

Clear thinking equaled clear action, a skill she learned from her mother. Daisy was pleased that her mother hadn't called her back. It meant she had faith in her daughter's judgment. That Chester didn't share the same type of faith was a bit unsettling for Daisy. His concern was tempered with aggression, something she didn't like.

She imagined that John Doe felt as if he was smack

between the proverbial rock and a hard place. In spite of all his troubles with amnesia, she knew he was a man she could trust. He showed careful thinking skills when he verbalized a concern about putting her in danger.

He wasn't waiting for someone to take care of him. He was simply regrouping after what could have been life-threatening injuries.

The multiple blows to his head could have caused more than temporary unconsciousness. The blows to his chest area could have caused internal injuries. All he had was amnesia. It was bad not to know who he was exactly, but it could have been a lot worse.

The big question she faced next was how to figure out who he was without arousing the suspicions and greater wrath of the people who beat him up in the first place.

Daisy looked at her notes. The timeline was skimpy. At this point in the investigation of John Doe's true identity, she had no doubts about his concern for her welfare, but concern and trust were separate issues.

He seemed like a nice guy. She believed he was innocent of any crime unless proven otherwise by police investigation. She just wasn't sure if she could trust him to give her all the facts of his memory reconstruction as they occurred.

Daisy thought about how smooth and confident John Doe was with women, the women at the emergency room and with herself, in spite of the dire circumstances that he found himself in, circumstances that put him squarely in a nest of strangers.

His smoothness, she decided, came from confidence. Like a cat slapped to the ground, he had somehow found the inner agility to land back on his feet. He hadn't been a pushover for Chester to shove around.

He'd given as good as he got, even though it had to hurt to put up a tough front when his body was banged up from head to foot.

It was that edge of controlled power in John Doe's smile and eyes that kept Daisy from thinking what happened to him was a random act of violence. That kind of controlled power, combined with his size and excellent physical condition, did not make him an easy target for random crime.

His terrible beating struck Daisy as a personal issue. Somebody somewhere didn't like John Doe. She bet someone he knew had it in for him. It was even possible that whoever beat him up cared enough about him to keep him alive. This idea made sense to her.

Powerful men made powerful enemies. A man as controlled under pressure as he was had to have a solid internal base of self-confidence, the kind of confidence engineered from birth in a trusting environment, not the kind manufactured by personal desire.

This was no Tony Robbins motivation disciple.

This man was a package deal. He had brawn, acted like he had brains, and was calm under pressure. Package deals were complex individuals. Daisy liked a complicated man. A complicated man had secrets, goals, dreams.

He had the kind of allure that kept an active woman like herself satisfied.

Just because Daisy kept her lifestyle simple didn't mean she liked a simple man. She was drawn to John Doe in more ways than a bleeding heart to a stray in need of rescue. Beaten-up and bruised, John Doe was still a force to be reckoned with.

Otherwise Chester wouldn't be so unsettled. He wouldn't be so unwilling to trust him, to aid an injured man.

John Doe wasn't the only one who was cool under pressure. She hadn't broken stride herself since finding the stranger in her compost pile. If she noted this about John Doe, he had to have noticed the same thing about her.

What he didn't know was that she didn't take every Tom, Dick, and Harry who ventured onto her property at face value. So far, everything about John Doe, from his dramatic arrival to his being a guest at her kitchen table, had taken them to a complex level of interpersonal relationships.

Some women might think she was crazy to take in a man the way she had. It was no stranger than owning a bed and breakfast and having a guest spend a night or two. Daisy didn't live in seclusion in some remote area of deep country, an area so remote that a man could do her bodily harm, even kill her, and nobody would know about it for days or weeks at a time.

She had a business that was open six days a week, delivery people she worked with, visiting friends and family, and of course there was Chester, her guy Friday. He, too, had been a rescue of Daisy's.

Chester had a degree in pharmacology and could get a job at just about any medical facility in the area. After he'd gotten his college degree, he'd found out pharmacology wasn't a field he wanted to be in for the rest of his life.

He had degrees and certificates up the ying-yang from Central University of Edmond and from Langston University, but no real practical work experience in his field. They had met at the local library in Guthrie.

He had been sitting in the magazine section, right in front of the *Southern Living* magazine Daisy wanted to get her hands on. She shared the table with him, and after a while they started talking. She offered him a job doing the odd lifting and hauling around the rose and garden shop. They'd been friends ever since.

There had been no trouble or discord between them until the arrival of John Doe. As she prepared for the garden club meeting, Daisy's mind was mostly on her injured guest. She wondered if he was getting any rest at all.

John Doe was resting by staying put in Daisy's home. He left the kitchen table to stare out the window. He saw that her lawn needed mowing. Mowing meant cutting things down, doing away with the ugly to get to the good.

When it came to the investigation into his true identity, getting to the good meant going to the police, sifting through countless missing persons reports, hoping one would match his description.

Somehow he knew he wasn't a criminal even though anyone could commit a crime for a powerful enough reason. For instance, a murder might be committed during an act of self-defense. He needed answers. He needed them quickly, judging by the amount of bruising on his body.

He grudgingly thanked Chester for a loaner of clothes but other than that, he'd decided not to push their tenuous truce. While Daisy was at work, he'd run a load of laundry. Running laundry made him wonder about his mother. He wondered if she was alive.

If she was alive, at least one person would wonder why he was missing. Hopefully, she would set into motion the wheels of discovering his whereabouts. In the meantime, he had to get moving. He needed to do something more than brood about his predicament.

The only problem was that his body was so stiff he felt like the Tin Man in *The Wizard of Oz* before Dorothy hooked him up with a can of oil. In this case, the can of oil was Daisy's generosity.

Without her generosity, John Doe figured he would probably be at the local police station, especially if Chester had any say in the matter. Chester told him before he left the last time that if he harmed Daisy in any way, it would be the last thing he ever did.

Daisy had just wanted him to rest, and rest he would. It was the only way he knew to regain his physical strength. His hostess deserved to be able to kick him out of her house as quickly as possible without feeling regret.

By rights, she should have left him at the hospital and told him good luck on her way out the glass sliding doors of the emergency room. She hadn't done that. He respected her for her level of commitment to a puzzle which challenged them both, the puzzle of his true identity.

He ran a palm down the back of his head. It didn't hurt the way it had this morning. Unbidden, an image flashed through his mind of a woman telling him, "Jump in the tub, son. There's nothing like a good soak to cure what ails you."

Alone in a stranger's house, John Doe realized he had a mother somewhere, a woman who cared about him, who would soon figure out that, like Dorothy, her son was a long way from home.

Seven

The garden club meeting at Daisy's Rose and Garden shop was a full house, complete with dazzling sales that resulted from so many people browsing through the merchandise.

Plywood shelves on two-by-fours were filled with companion plants, the kinds of flowers that grew well with roses. As the customers waited until the official start of the informal garden club meeting, a social event that was well anticipated under normal circumstances, they filled their hands with plants to take home later.

There were many companion plants to choose from. In dark green one-gallon containers, Daisy grew hollyhock, baby's-breath, primrose, and a variety of geraniums. In small six-pack containers, she raised plants that thrived for one season only; the petunia, candytuft, and forget-me-nots were receiving a lot of attention, especially the plants she grew in the color blue.

Other than the premeeting browse session Daisy had expected, very little else was turning out to be normal about the flow of the garden club meeting. On this warm May night, an electric air of energy highlighted the evening.

Instead of the meeting being routine, this gathering of old friends felt more like a garden party.

It was usually an evening conducted under more relaxed conditions by women who came together as much for casual gossip as they did for gardening advice from a woman well respected within the small Guthrie community. Still, Daisy made every effort to ignore the steady buzz of conversation about John Doe.

At its height, the garden club roster was twenty members strong. With busy personal schedules, Daisy considered a gathering of ten members an excellent crowd. The fact that all twenty members showed up tonight suggested that nothing about the meeting would be business as usual.

She didn't expect too much of the meeting to be about gardening, but at least she was prepared with tips on composting. In a roundabout way, the first question of the evening had a slight bearing on the topic.

After all, for a little while, John Doe had been an ingredient in her compost pile.

Cinnamon Hartfeld spoke first. She was a four-foot-three-inch tall, pleasantly plump high achiever. For the last three years, Cinnamon had run a successful antique shop on Harrison Street, a small business which specialized in Victorian underwear.

"So Daisy," Cinnamon said, her voice slightly high with excitement, "where is your mystery guest?"

Daisy decided to have a little fun with her old friend. They had been junior high school cheerleaders together. One thing Cinnamon couldn't stand was a secret, especially a secret with a bit of scandal thrown into it. Cinnamon enjoyed getting to the bottom of a secret almost as much as she enjoyed getting to the bottom of a family heirloom trunk filled with Victorian clothes and other keepsakes. "Who?" Daisy asked, feigning innocence. "Chester?"

Cinnamon tossed the chin-length braided extensions on her head. She was not about to be distracted by Daisy's stalling tactics. "Don't get me started, girlfriend. Where is the man you found knocked out in your garden?"

Cinnamon's bold question opened a flood of conversation. Potted perennial plants were set down. The last two customers at the petunia shelf found seats together. The meeting had officially started; all attention was directed at Daisy.

Raucous shouts of "Yeah, where is he?" "Bring him on!" and "Tell us what happened!" rocked the air.

Daisy waved her carefully prepared paper with tips on composting into the electrified air. Hardly anybody glanced at the waving piece of paper. Nobody wanted to hear a word she said about gardening advice.

Everyone wanted to hear about John Doe.

"I heard he is fine." Zenith Braxton pronounced the word *fine* like *foyne*. Zenith's mother had been Daisy's baby-sitter throughout grade school while Daisy's mom had worked as a cook at Miss Carolyn's Territorial House on North Division Street.

Besides blue-plate specials like tender steak and seasoned fries smothered in homemade gravy, Daisy's mother specialized in quality baked desserts, treats that were often served as house favorites.

Zenith's mother *also* made tasty desserts. Zenith's mother *also* specialized in plain good cooking.

As children, Zenith and Daisy often argued about whose mom cooked the best. Daisy recognized the same needling tone in Zenith's voice that she remembered from their grade-school arguments.

She grinned, something she realized she'd been doing a lot since John Doe's arrival. She didn't feel tense about the subject. Her relaxed body language showed off her positive attitude. Daisy eyed her friend with a teasing look. "He's also tall, dark, and mysterious."

The room buzzed with shouted questions.

"How can he be fine when he's all beat up?"

"Let us see him!"

"Let us judge for ourselves!"

Daisy waved her paper one last time. "Ladies, unless you want to look at the exhibition roses or talk about composting or anything else to do with gardening, we'll have to adjourn the meeting."

Cinnamon's laugh was lusty. "That fine, huh?"

Lewd laughter joined the chorus of "Bring 'im on, Daisy." The rest of the comments were bachelorette-party style.

Daisy directed a look at her friend. The pitch of her voice was loud enough to be heard by every woman in the garden shop. "He's that fine, Cinnamon, but I also don't want to make him uptight. He's got a lot on his mind right now."

Zenith said, "Please. I heard the man lost his mind." Her look was coy. She hadn't grown out of the habit of baiting Daisy. They both enjoyed the rivalry, a contest of wills that stemmed largely from being raised like sisters.

Both women had mothers who believed in the village concept of child rearing. Compliments were handed out to each girl as easy as discipline. Zenith's mother had been

as handy with a switch to Daisy's legs as she had been
with her own daughter's legs.

The village concept was in effect at the meeting. What
one woman found, the other women examined as a col-
lective. "Let us help you find his"—Zenith's pause was
suggestive—"mind for him."

Daisy sailed the paper on composting to the countertop.
Composting was a staple for any serious gardener. Despite
all the bawdy talk, the room was filled with serious gardeners, people who would normally welcome the chance
to talk about soil improvement with an expert.

She would save the topic for some other meeting.

It was at their suggestion that she'd started the gardening club in the first place. After two years of successful
meetings, Daisy felt comfortable speaking plainly to her
guests. "You can't help him find anything."

"Tsk, tsk. You selfish girl," Miss Myrtle said. "Who
knows what one of us might have seen in town. If we get
a look at the fella you're hiding from us, maybe somebody
in here will recognize him and can help. Didn't your
mama ever teach you to take good help when you can get
it?"

Cinnamon said, "Take the help, girl. Let us in on your
juicy little secret." She looked around the shop as if he
might be hiding behind one of the display racks. "Wherever
your little secret is."

Daisy sighed. Even though John Doe was a stranger to
her, she felt he deserved to keep out of the public eye if
he wanted to do so. She didn't think he stood a chance
of success. "How can John Doe be a secret when everybody in the room knows about him?"

"John Doe? So it's true," Zenith said. "The man really

doesn't know his own name after all. That's tough. Let me check him out, Daisy. Maybe I can help him."

Daisy shook her head, half in jest, half in exasperation. She really did want to keep John Doe out of the hot seat of twenty questions. She had a feeling she would be as successful as she had been with the composting tips. "You guys are scandalous."

"And you think you aren't?" Cinnamon asked. "You've got yourself some"—she paused as she scrambled for just the right words—"exotic stuff tucked away in your house, but you aren't willing to share how you got it."

"I run a garden shop, Cinnamon, not a gossip shop."

Miss Myrtle made a face. "Since when?"

"Since now." Daisy headed to the cash register. It was time to end the meeting.

At the end of the meeting, some women left right away. Other women browsed one last time. Tonight, everyone took Daisy's move to the cash register as the signal it was meant to be: The garden club meeting was officially adjourned.

The conversation was full of sighs. Several women grabbed purchases and handbags as they prepared to leave the garden shop. Those same women stopped cold when John Doe arrived on the scene.

As soon as he saw all activity come to an instant stop, conversation included, John Doe recognized he'd made a huge mistake. With so many interested female eyes on him, he felt like meat on the dinner table: hot, tender, and tasty.

While the expressions of some women were neutral, a few studied John Doe as if he really were one of Daisy's prized experimental roses: bright, bold, and one-of-a-kind.

Daisy had the reputation for helping anybody at least once. If she got burned, she left the person alone. But this was no ordinary stray she'd found in her garden.

She laughed at the stunned look on John Doe's face. "Come on, big guy. We were supposed to discuss the dos and don'ts of composting. But since you were discovered in the compost pile, everyone wanted to talk about that instead. As I'm sure you can imagine, it's been a lively discussion. A whole lot of territory has been covered in the last half hour. Good thing you just got here. We're about to shut down for the night."

He rolled his shoulders to loosen them up along with his attitude. These were Daisy's friends, people he intended to be kind to no matter what was said or done within the next few minutes. Still, the silence was unnerving.

A stout woman with bright fuschia lipstick and silver hoop earrings nearly to her shoulders kept squeezing her hands open and closed as if she wanted to squeeze John Doe. He felt absolutely naked when he said to Daisy, "I believe you."

He was sure the women were all nice and friendly, but it was Saturday night; these ladies were having a good time teasing Daisy. Perhaps it was their way of letting him know she had friends in Guthrie, friends who wanted to check him out from head to foot.

Daisy pulled him close to stand beside her. It was so quiet, she heard the hum of the overhead lights. "Ladies of the garden club, meet John Doe."

The hand squeezer whistled at him as if he'd scored a home run at a baseball game. The whistle was loud and long and explosive. He nodded his head in acknowledgment of what he considered a call of rally to the wolves.

"Ladies," he said to the room at large, "it's nice to meet you."

Instantly, questions began to fly in his direction as if he were the spokesman at a press conference.

"Does your eye hurt? It looks bad."

"What kind of food do you like to eat?"

"Are you homesick?"

"How long will you be staying?"

"Will you help Daisy around the shop?"

"When you get tired of staying with Daisy, Little Boy Blue, you just come on over to my place."

The last remark was said with such sexual undertones that John Doe couldn't help but laugh. "You guys are something else."

"You too, honey," said Miss Myrtle. "You too."

Daisy couldn't believe the situation could get any worse, but it did.

Chester showed up.

He charged into the meeting like wind blowing open a front door. To Daisy's astute gaze, he looked madder than a cat that had just missed the mouse. She knew full well he was there to check on John Doe, who was supposed to be resting and wasn't.

Two men vying for the same young woman created a rowdy night no one present at the garden club meeting was likely to forget anytime soon, a delicious thought for Daisy. It was all she could do not to grin just thinking about it.

The rowdy night would create more gossip. All the gossip going on around her, right down to Chester showing up to promptly get into a glaring match with John Doe, would go a long way toward boosting business sales the next day.

Miss Myrtle would tell her crowd of friends. Cinnamon and Zenith would tell their friends. When word got around to Chester about how he was letting another man step on his turf, then Chester would get into a discussion with his friends. Daisy felt elated on the one hand, appalled on the other.

She felt appalled because now John Doe, a guest in her home, would no longer have privacy as he healed from his injuries. She felt elated because so much conversation meant people would bandy ideas around regarding how he ended up in her garden in the first place. Overall, the gossip could open a lead into John Doe's secret identity.

When the gossip spread through Guthrie, someone's memory might be triggered, which was actually a good thing. Even though he never complained, John Doe had to be miserable not knowing his own name.

He made no secret it drove him crazy not to have money for his own essentials. Chester had loaned him an extra running suit—very grudgingly, and it was just as poorly accepted. Daisy had no problem dispensing his toiletry items, but John Doe had trouble accepting them.

When she'd handed him a red toothbrush and a fresh tube of Crest toothpaste, he scowled. His wrinkled look of displeasure at that time played second to the scowl he threw at Chester right now.

Daisy was glad John Doe felt offended. His irritated look meant he had pride, a trait she valued in a man. Like companion plants for roses, pride made the perfect companion to conscience. Both attributes, pride and conscience, reinforced her opinion she had done the right thing by lending him a helping hand.

If the tables were turned, if it was she who was found with a knot on her head, penniless, and without identification, she could only hope that somebody would stick a hand and a heart out to help her as she had helped John Doe. She called her style of generosity simple human kindness.

She wished she could say the same about Chester.

There was nothing simple or generous about Chester's expression or his attitude. Just like Daisy, he knew all the women present at the meeting. It was obvious he shared John Doe's discomfort about the garden club members' close scrutiny. She figured he was ready to explode with anger—at John Doe for being on the scene and at the women for making him feel embarrassed. Chester liked to stay in the background, which was the reason he never ran the register. The work he did for Daisy was strictly manual labor.

Daisy laughed outright when he grabbed John Doe by the shoulder and said, "Man, let's get to steppin'."

John Doe had already started walking away from Daisy's side. "For once," he muttered to Chester, "you're talking my language."

The lively background chatter lowered as the men made their hasty exit, but the spirited conversation never stopped. On his way out the garden shop door, John Doe felt a pinch on his butt.

One thing was for certain: If the people who had beaten him up and dumped him in Daisy's garden were still around, they would soon learn that he was alive and well.

He had a lot more on his mind than aches and pains or

a little embarrassment over a few catcalls and wolf whistles. He had Daisy's safety to consider. In that regard, he and Chester were in total agreement.

Eight

Outside, the men stopped at Chester's Dodge Ram. For several minutes, each man was silent, content to keep his own counsel for the moment. The first man to speak would set the tone of their encounter. John Doe had no problem waiting for Chester's volley.

While he waited, John Doe recalled his thoughts from that morning as he left Daisy's shop to get some sleep in her house. Worried about Daisy, he couldn't sleep. He thought of her constantly, his feelings shifting from gratitude to deep attraction.

In a short time, she'd made a powerful impact on his life. John Doe enjoyed the fine feeling that something terrific was just around the corner for them if they dared explore the wonder together.

In Daisy's relaxed, carefree environment, John Doe was struck by the irony he'd been beaten and left for dead in her garden. Daisy's lifestyle was the opposite of violence.

She was the kind of woman John Doe could easily serve and protect with all his heart, something he'd felt like doing from the beginning. She just didn't know it; Chester did.

As he'd laid on the bed in Daisy's guest bedroom, trying to get some rest, John Doe had brooded, his dislike of Chester Whitcomb the source of his deep, disturbing thoughts. In his own way, Chester had wooed Daisy relentlessly, using weapons John Doe had no way of matching, the weapons of shared history and personal knowledge.

It was Chester's possessive attitude that troubled John Doe the most. He worried Chester might hurt Daisy in a fit of rage, violence rooted in unrequited love. Of one thing John Doe was certain: Daisy didn't love the other man beyond platonic friendship.

Whether either of them realized it or not, her behavior had shifted toward Chester; she was edgy. John Doe worried her new awareness might push Chester into frustrated aggression against her.

As Daisy had said, her life was fairly peaceful and basic. She had a profitable business which didn't stress her out. She was fun to be with and to talk to. She asked for little beyond simple courtesy and respect. John Doe's being a guest in her home was an example of this type of live-and-let-live philosophy. Had Chester allowed the aggressive side of his personality to dominate, Daisy probably wouldn't have kept him around.

In turn, had Chester truly been easygoing, he wouldn't have taken an instant dislike and distrust to John Doe. Men with big chips on their shoulders were often men without clear consciences.

Regardless, John Doe felt Daisy and Chester were at the limits of a relationship probably set within vague but comfortable bounds. She had a reliable source of muscle at her disposal; he was able to work near the woman he loved.

Perhaps now, with the advent of John Doe's arrival and the shift in Daisy's attention, Chester felt his nonthreatening approach had been a tactical error. Maybe Chester thought Daisy considered him harmless, a reason she put up with his rude behavior. Daisy attributed his rudeness to simple but unnecessary jealousy, when in truth jealousy was never a simple issue. The fact that Chester barely controlled his feelings of rivalry only reinforced his anger. For John Doe, these warnings signaled trouble ahead.

That morning, a low-key dread had forced John Doe to leave the soft, chintz-covered comfort of Daisy's guest bedroom. He was restless, tired of hurting, tired of waiting for his memory to click in with no missing links in his thinking process.

He wanted to get on with his life.

He'd strode into the backyard, its focal point a small white gazebo. The roses around the gazebo were less than three feet tall. Like most of the roses in Daisy's gardens, these were lush with green foliage, many of them scattered with blooms.

The gazebo roses were dusky pink, the color of new love, of new hope. John Doe had found himself hoping fervently that no harm would come Daisy's way between now and the return of his memory.

Somehow, he didn't think so.

John Doe had kicked into action; brooding would get him nowhere. In less than a minute he'd left the beauty of Daisy's garden to walk briskly down the road in an effort to work the sore kinks out of his body. His battered face was healing nicely, although a scar would remain near his left temple.

He needed his full strength even if he never regained his full memory. His days as a guest in Daisy's house had a number to them. Beyond a few days, a guest became a freeloader, something John Doe refused to be.

One thing he hadn't lost in the fight for his identity was his pride. It was probably pride that kept Chester from making a scene at the garden club meeting. Despite their differences, at the moment, the silence between Chester and John Doe was amicable.

The night was beautiful. The native redbuds, Oklahoma's state tree, were in bloom, the flowers pink, the leaves shaped like purple-hued hearts.

Daisy had placed a short grove of redbuds on either side of her pea gravel driveway. The trees were thirteen to fifteen feet tall, but slender and fine-branched enough to allow sun to penetrate through the leaves. In turn, the sun bathed the double-bloom impatiens that lined the driveway.

Chester pulled a supple leaf off the redbud branch nearest his right shoulder. He was the first man to speak, his tone aggressive despite the easy way he moved about Daisy's property. "I've been watching you."

John Doe was equally cold. He, too, moved with ease over the property. He'd studied it from the windows and during his brief walks to rebuild his strength. "I know. It's obvious you don't trust Daisy to do what she feels is right."

Chester ripped the purple leaf he held too tightly. Frustrated, he tossed the remnants to the ground. "My feelings for Daisy are none of your business."

John Doe pushed Chester to the boiling point when he said, "She's my business as long as I'm staying in her house." He pressed Chester in order to discover the underlying reason for his outrageous attitude.

"You won't be here much longer." The statement sounded exactly like the threat it was meant to be.

"I hope that's true, Whitcomb. But I promise you one

thing. When I leave, it won't be because you made me. The arrangement I have is between Daisy and me."

"Daisy is innocent."

John Doe never once removed his gaze from his opponent's face. "An interesting choice of words, Whitcomb. I never said she was guilty of anything. Are you?"

Chester stilled. "Am I what?"

"Guilty."

Chester kicked at the pale gray rocks on the ground. "I've got nothing to hide. This is my turf. You're the one who's out of place."

"I'm not hiding," John Doe clarified. "I've got amnesia."

"So you say."

"Yeah. So I say. As does the doctor. You were there."

Chester rested an elbow on the tailgate of his truck. The tension in his voice denied the confidence he sought to portray with his nonchalant pose. "Dr. Randal isn't a psychiatrist. I still say you're faking."

"What advantage or reason would I have to fake amnesia?" John Doe countered. He was totally serious.

"There's a reason for everything."

"Funny. You don't look like a philosopher."

Off came the elbow from the tailgate of the truck. Chester's fists were curled tight and ready for action. His voice had a demon-mean rasp to it. "Don't bait me."

"Then get out of my face."

"You have no right to order me around." Chester's rasp of fury remained intact. A vein pulsed across his right temple.

"You have no right to detain me, either, but that's exactly what you're doing right now." John Doe leaned on Chester's truck as if he had nothing but time on his hands. His tone of voice was neutral, as was the expression on his face.

"You're not a cop, Whitcomb. You're not Daisy's husband or even her boyfriend. You're Daisy's employee. You have about as much right to be here as I do."

"You have no rights."

"Oh, yes I do. We're both here because she wants us here. Do you really want her to know you're harassing me?"

Chester hated John Doe for being correct. He didn't want Daisy to see him arguing with her latest stray. Still, he couldn't resist one more dig. "I've been to the Guthrie police."

"Good."

If Chester had meant to shock John Doe, he'd failed miserably. The injured man shifted his weight against the truck. "I expect the police to be involved. My identity will turn up eventually."

"You can't stay here indefinitely!" The lid was off Chester's boiling animosity.

"I know."

"What are your plans?"

John Doe wanted to laugh at Chester's dogged persistence in getting rid of him. He never wavered in his opposition, never altered his opinion. His tenacity sent warning bells clanging in John Doe's mind. "Are you asking me as Daisy's friend or for your own twisted reasons?"

"There's nothing twisted about my interest in you. Like I keep saying, you don't belong here. Your being here is a mistake."

"Mistake," John Doe repeated, his tone thoughtful. "An interesting word you've got there, Whitcomb."

Sheer suspicion dominated the energy coming from Chester. "What are you talking about?"

"My being here is a fluke. Actually, it's more like a stroke of fortune for me. However, you think it's a mistake I turned up in Daisy's garden. You've got my wheels turning, Whitcomb."

Chester stalked off. "Later for you, John . . . Doe."

"Later."

Three steps from the truck door, Chester turned back. "Don't get me wrong, I still think you know more than you're saying. I think whoever kicked your ass the first time is lined up to kick your ass again. But if you hurt one hair on Daisy's head, I promise, John . . . Doe, I'll break your head for real this time. You won't get away with a simple concussion."

John Doe's eyebrow shifted into an arc of feigned dismay. "I'm scared, Whitcomb. Really scared."

"You should be."

John Doe snorted. He didn't know a lot about the last twenty-four hours, but he did know he hated idle threats. *"You* should be afraid of Daisy. If you love her as much as I think you do, you ought to give her the respect she deserves by trusting her to make the right decisions about how she spends her time and shares her home."

Chester shot forward, fist raised.

John Doe sidestepped his fist. "I want nothing more than to bust you upside the head, Whitcomb, but I've got too much respect for Daisy to upset her. Not only that, she'd feel embarrassed in front of her friends if we started a brawl right here in her driveway. Get a grip on yourself."

Chester's chest heaved as if he'd just run a mile against the wind. "Don't talk to me about respect."

"I won't talk to you unless I have to talk to you. You've got a hot head and a quick hand, Whitcomb. I don't trust that about you."

"Don't talk to me about trust, you bastard." Chester's voice was full of suppressed hatred for the man who lived in Daisy's house, however temporary the arrangement.

John Doe's voice was solid granite. "Shove off, Whitcomb. You don't mean squat to me. If it wasn't for Daisy, I wouldn't look at you twice. I don't have time for hotheads."

Mad as a two-year-old who couldn't get his way, Chester threw back his head, opened his mouth, and roared. Even the birds scattered from the trees.

Daisy heard him, too. "Chester? Is that you?"

It took all Chester's will to subdue his rage, to control his breathing, to get a grip on sanity. He hated to admit it, but John Doe was right. Daisy would be embarrassed by a fight, especially when she had customers.

"Chester?" they heard her calling in the distance.

Understanding Chester's struggle for composure, John Doe laughed. The laugh was as ugly as the bruises on his injured face. "Go, Chester. Step and fetch it."

Chester threw a punch at John Doe's face.

He aimed for the swollen eye.

John Doe ducked and threw a left hook into Chester's stomach. He shoved him to the ground. "Back off."

Chester's eyes bored holes into John Doe's body. Hatred radiated off him in shimmering waves of red heat. "You're gonna pay for this, John . . . Doe. Promise."

Nine

It was Saturday afternoon. As Daisy had predicted, some of the women at the garden club meeting had talked to some of the men in town who had talked to friends of Chester's about John Doe stepping on Chester's turf by staying with his woman.

Those very same people knew Daisy wasn't Chester's woman—at least not officially. Knowing she and Chester weren't a couple wouldn't stop the matchmakers in town from adding one young and healthy woman to one young and healthy man to equal one young and attractive couple.

Some of the men who gossiped in town figured the main reason Chester Whitcomb stuck around Daisy's Rose and Garden Shop hauling dirt and transplanting roses day in and day out was to get into Daisy's pants.

Out of the male friends who had talked to Chester after the women returned home from the garden club meeting, three of the men were with the Guthrie Police Department. Being friends first and law officers second, those friends were less than objective in their observance of Daisy's right to privacy, Spud Gurber in particular.

Like Dr. Randal, Spud Gurber didn't give too much thought to the rules of confidentiality when it came to Daisy. Nobody in Logan County who knew her at all wanted to see her taken advantage of by a stranger with an eye still swollen from a beating nobody saw. This was Spud's excuse for being neighborly.

The way the garden club women and Chester's friends figured, Chester ought to be upset. He ought to be pushing to get the stranger out of his hair and off Daisy's property. The fact that what Daisy did on her own time was entirely her business was a minor technicality.

In real life, people were nosy and not necessarily nice.

That Sunday afternoon, Spud found Chester spreading mulch around the grandiflora shrub roses.

Spud followed him through the section of tall and bushy Montezuma roses, the Pink Parfaits, the blackish-red Scarlet Knights, and the salmon-pink Queen Elizabeths. As a group, the roses smelled fantastic.

Spud fingered the white plastic tag on a Queen Elizabeth rosebush. Standing alone, the smell of the flower was mild, but he stuck his nose in the center of a globe-shaped bloom and smiled anyway.

It was a sly smile, Spud's prelude to making trouble. "Daisy must think she's lack this rose she's got growing here."

Chester grimaced over the pronunciation of the word *like* as the word *lack*. "I'm sure you can't wait to tell me."

"I'm sure you is one-hunnit-percent correct, too."

Spud put a fresh dab of his favorite tobacco chew in his mouth. He had bought a fresh pack from Wal-Mart the night before, so he relished the full freshness of the new pack. He used his tongue to slide the tobacco into the pocket of his right cheek where it could get nice and wet.

He wasn't supposed to use chew on the job, but he

justified his action by telling himself he was on break. "I say she thinks she's a Queen Elizabeth because she thinks she's so high and mighty."

"You can't possibly be talking about Daisy," Chester argued. "She's totally down to earth."

"Then why ain't she the one spreading mulch 'stead of you?"

"This is heavy work."

Spud snickered. "This is busy work. I've seen Daisy do it on her own too much to think it's a job she don't feel qualified to do. No suh, I'd say Daisy just got herself a mind to keep you out of the way of her and John Doe. Ain't he in the house in the AC and ain't you the one out here sweating and carrying on?"

"Shut up, Spud."

"Hee, hee." Spit. "Hee, hee."

"Go on back to work, Spud."

"My pleasure." Spud's tone was that of a conspirator. "But first, don't you wanna know what Zenith's mama said about Little Boy Blue?"

Chester stopped spreading mulch to stare at Spud. "Little who?"

"Boy Blue. You know, John Doe."

"Zenith's mama wasn't even at the garden club meeting yesterday, Spud."

"That John Doe fella got your head all turned around. *Zenith* was at the meeting, you fool. You know Zenith tells her mama everything there is to tell and then makes up something to tell her mama when she runs out of gossip between talk shows."

"You are way worse than Zenith, Spud. Way worse."

"Whatever." Spit. "Anyway, Zenith's mama said that

John Doe had stopped at Sonic for some cheddar-cheese peppers, a Route 44 root beer, and a grilled cheese samich."

Chester dumped more shredded cypress mulch from the wheelbarrow onto the floor of the flower bed. He spread the mulch with a vengeance. *"Sandwich,* Spud. Can't you say *sandwich* instead of *samich,* for crying out loud?"

"I had the same schooling you did in Guthrie, but *I"*— Spud pointed at his chest— *"I* went on to Oklahoma University right in good old Norman, Oklahoma, and studied on crime. I got me a degree I can *use.* You're the one spreading mulch for the Queen Elizabeths."

"All right, all right. Let's not get into a pissing contest."

"Damn straight." Spit. "Just because you talk a litta better than I do don't mean I ain't got no education. I got me a degree *and* a good job. You don't see me breaking a sweat over a woman who ain't even close to giving me the time of day. Daisy is playing you for a fool, man. A deep country fool."

Chester threw his heavy-duty rake down. "You wouldn't be talking so tough if you didn't have that badge on, and you know it." He turned his palms into fists. "If you didn't have that badge on I'd do what I want to do and punch you in the face."

Spit. Spit. "And I done come all the way out here to tell you that when Zenith's mama talked to her friend Miss Myrtle, who by the way was also at the meeting, Miss Myrtle remembered seeing a black Impala down on Oklahoma Street at that new Mexican restaurant. You know the one, La Fuente Grande or La Fuente or La . . . something lack that. You know the one. The food is good."

Chester's interest peaked. "Yeah. I know the one. Can anybody on the grapevine remember who was driving the black Impala?"

"Two men. Neither one of 'em was John Doe."

"What was he driving at Sonic?"

"Nothing. He was sitting at that new round picnic table Sonic put out after they renovated the place. As I said, John Doe didn't have no car. That's how Zenith's mama knew he had cheddar peppers. She loves cheddar peppers but she ain't been able to eat 'em lately on account of she been sick."

"What are the police doing about this officially?"

Both men whipped around at the sound of Daisy's voice. Neither of them had heard her approach, but her question definitely got their undivided attention.

At the same time, both men said, "Uh-oh."

Daisy put her hands on her hips. "Spud? Shouldn't you be cruising down Division looking for something to get into besides a Daylight Donut?"

Spud started to spit, but changed his mind when he saw the look on Daisy's face. She looked ready to whop him upside the head for stirring Chester up. Chester still had his palms balled into fists.

Spud decided to stay off the subject of Chester. "Girl, you know dang well that cops eating donuts all the time is a stereotype."

"I expect you to uphold the laws of justice, Spud Gurber, not the laws of gossip according to the garden club."

Chester stepped to her side. "She's right, Spud. You ought to be cruising down Division looking for clues."

Daisy and Spud spoke at the same time: "Shut up, Chester!"

Daisy wagged a finger at Spud. "Just because we go all the way back to first grade doesn't mean you can treat me any different from any other regular citizen in this town. If I were a tourist you'd be trying harder to find out who John Doe is instead of gossiping with your buddy Chester here."

Spud was indignant. "I am not gossiping."

"Okay then, Officer Gurber. Does spreading half truths and flat-out lies sound better than gossiping?"

Chester rallied. "Now, Daisy."

"Now, Daisy my foot," she countered. "I'm tempted to solve this missing identity case of John Doe's on my own. I'd probably have better luck."

Spud was already shaking his head. "As a friend, I care about what happens to you, Daisy. I just want Chester here to have a heads-up about what he's dealing with. If you get hurt, then I'll have to kick Chester's—"

Daisy raised a hand in the halt position. "Chester better start worrying about me kicking his behind."

Spud snickered. Chester glared.

"I'm serious, Chester," Daisy explained. "I need a friend right now, not an enemy."

He unclenched his fists. "I could never be your enemy."

This time, it was John Doe who surprised the group. He wore his own running suit. After a good night's sleep and several cups of Daisy's cure-all chamomile tea, he felt better than the day before. "Then stop acting like one."

Chester snatched the garden rake off the ground. He brandished the rake at John Doe like a soldier in the film *The 13th Warrior* starring Antonio Banderas. Daisy might have laughed if the situation weren't so serious.

Spud turned official. His voice was stern. "Think, man."

Chester had eyes only for John Doe, but he spoke to Spud. "Everything was fine between me and Daisy until he showed up. He's nothing but trouble."

Spud stepped to the hand that held the rake. "He ain't committed no crime, either. If you go at him with this rake, I'll haul ya into the station. Keep your head tight, brother."

John Doe turned to Daisy. "Let's go to the house."

Chester charged.

John Doe was ready for him. He snatched the rake with one hand. He shoved Chester back with the other.

Chester roared and charged again.

John Doe swept him off his feet with one foot.

Chester was incensed. He jumped to his feet, then lowered his body into a crouch. He bared his teeth. Just before he launched himself at John Doe, Spud whipped out his billy club. "Chester. Chill."

Chester's mouth fell open. "You'd hit me with that?"

Spud was taking no guff. "If I have to clock you upside the head with it, yes suh, I will hit you with it."

"I thought you were my friend!"

Spud cared about law and order. "Lack you said, I got a badge on, and that means I'm here on official police business."

Chester still couldn't believe it. "You'd hit me because of him? You don't even know him."

"Ain't got to know him. I just gotta know wrong when I see it. Lack I said, he ain't committed no crime. You don't have cause to hit him."

Chester was breathing so hard, Daisy thought he might hyperventilate. She placed a hand on his chest.

He backed off. "Don't touch me."

She was deeply offended.

Despite Chester's rude behavior since the stranger's arrival, Daisy still had affection for him. Because of that affection, she found it hard to stay mad. She moved toward Chester, but John Doe kept her from going.

He made her stand by his side by placing a hand on her arm. In doing so, he signaled to Chester that he challenged his role as defender. Chester turned red. He went from breathing too fast to not breathing at all.

John Doe said, "I think you'd better go." This, after day two on the premises. John Doe figured he had nerve, but at least he had Daisy's best interests at heart. He wasn't so sure about Chester Whitcomb.

Spud agreed. "I'll walk you out, Chester."

Chester didn't blink for ten seconds. "I don't believe this."

Daisy watched him go with a funny mixture of sadness and relief. "I don't believe it, either."

She had seen Spud and Chester in different lights. She had always taken Spud half seriously. They had known each other forever, but when she really thought about it, he had to do more than write reports, control crowds, and answer emergency calls. She'd never thought about him conducting an investigation, let alone having anything to say about John Doe's missing identity. Spud didn't just stop crime, he prevented it from happening in the first place.

Stopping Chester from lashing out at John Doe meant he took the law seriously. Spud could have easily let Chester hit John Doe and stepped aside while the men fought. She respected Spud for doing his job by maintaining order.

From now on, she would consider him in a better light, not just as a means of controlling traffic when the stoplights downtown went out of whack. It was Chester who was out of whack, and it was Chester who had been controlled with a brief show of force and a few well-chosen words.

John Doe turned her to face him. "Chester is in love with you."

She scrunched her nose in mockery. "We don't have that kind of relationship. It's been kindness and friendship on my part. He's my employee, for God's sake."

"He can't help it, Daisy."

Her nose was still scrunched. "What do you mean he can't help it?"

John Doe looked her up and down. Even with her chin smudged with gardening soil and her face free of makeup, she was beautiful. "You're adorable, Daisy. If I were in Chester's place, I'd have fallen in love with you, too."

She smacked him on the shoulder. "Get outta here."

They walked to the house together. It was after six P.M., so the garden shop was closed. "Some day soon I'll leave, Daisy. But there's one thing I want to be sure and do before I go."

"What?"

He stopped walking. "This." He lifted her chin with his finger. Softly, he kissed her lips.

His tone was gentle. "Thank you for everything. I'll always remember you. No matter what happens, no matter where I go from here, I'll always be thankful I landed under your greenhouse and not somebody else's. I didn't know a greenhouse could be so small. Until meeting you, I never thought about a greenhouse at all."

She licked her lips. Her mouth felt dry. Her body felt hot. She wondered if he kissed her softly because his lips were tender from his beating or if he kissed her tender so as not to scare her off.

She wanted him to kiss her again. Instead of asking for a kiss, she said, "You mean, you wouldn't have wanted to land in Zenith's garden? She specializes in miniature roses. She's got about six hundred of them."

"Six hundred!"

"That's why she specializes in minis. She could plant six hundred more and get away with it in her yard."

"But six hundred?"

They resumed their walk to the house. They sat on the top step of the back porch, its roof shaded by an old willow tree. "Aside from Mr. Dillingsworth, Zenith is one of my best customers."

John Doe winced as he spread his legs in front of him. "Speaking of customers, I'll be helping you around the house and garden until I leave."

"That isn't necessary."

He disagreed. "Pride makes it necessary. I have to work in order to face myself in the mirror."

She thought perhaps painkillers were making him feel more like his former self, whoever that was. "You're still sore."

He stared into her eyes as if she were a living angel on earth. "I'm alive. Because of your generosity, I have nothing to complain about, Daisy."

She had learned quickly that it was a waste of time to argue with John Doe. "What would you do?"

"Finish spreading that mulch, for one thing."

"Chester will have a fit."

"True. But you still need your mulch spread." When she opened her mouth to protest, he stopped her with a finger on her lips. "I can handle Chester."

His finger had been against her lips only briefly, but she still felt his touch. Her entire body tingled in awareness. She returned his dark, unreadable gaze. "I believe you."

"And Daisy?"

"Yeah?" She couldn't believe how breathless she sounded.

"I think you're one heck of a woman."

"Are you flirting with me?" she whispered.

"Absolutely."

She turned away from him to study the trees in the distance. There were peach trees, apple trees, plum trees, and native cedar trees. She finally said, "You might have a wife somewhere, so don't start something you can't finish."

"I don't have a wife."

She stared at him a long time. The stare was the searching, measuring look of an intelligent woman. "How in the world could you know if you have a wife or not?"

His response was quick. "I don't have marks on my ring finger. If I were married to a woman I'd want to hang on to my ring."

There were other reasons besides a show of fidelity that a man might skip wearing his wedding ring. "Maybe you outgrew your ring, John Doe, or maybe it got in the way of your work."

He was shaking his head before she finished her sentence. "No. It's like not being able to take charity from you. Some things I just know. Trust me, Daisy. I don't have a wife waiting for me."

Daisy was kind, not gullible. "You might not have a wife or significant other, but you do have a life somewhere. Thanks to Spud, I realize the police might not be the help I'd like them to be. You need to get back to where you belong."

"You're right."

Daisy snapped her fingers. "I've got an idea." She stood on the top porch step so that she could face John Doe. "Let's do our own investigation. Me and you."

His expression was closed. "Together as in I do the investigating and you brainstorm with me at the end of the day."

She slapped her hands on her hips. "I'm not a coward."

"No. A coward would have left me in the compost pile."

She continued as if he hadn't spoken. "Besides, I'm the only person who cares about finding the truth anyway. You need somebody at your back, the way Cutie Pie has my back." She stuck out her hand. "Deal?"

He stared at her hand a long time. She was bold, fearless when she had someone to rescue. He needed to keep an eye on her. While he was protecting her from the bad guys, who was going to protect him from falling in love with her?

Chester.

The idea made him smile. Chester would rather break his legs and dump him in Zenith's miniature rose garden than see him end up with Daisy. After two days in her company, John Doe could understand why. She was delightful. She had no hidden agenda. She kept things simple, uncomplicated.

"Are you gonna take my hand or what?" she demanded.

He finally took her hand. "You've got a deal, Daisy Rogers." Besides, he figured, it was the best way he knew to keep tabs on her.

As far as John Doe was concerned, Chester wasn't doing a good job of protecting her. If she were his woman, no man, injured or not, would be staying ten feet from her let alone sleeping under the same roof with her.

Chester didn't deserve her.

"Partners."

She grinned. "Partners."

John Doe sat on the top step of Daisy's porch and knew he was in trouble. With her staring down into his face, her eyes shining with purpose, he knew he was falling in love, a man who didn't know his own name, a man whose interpretation of the world was deeply influenced by a woman with a tremendous ability to give of herself unconditionally.

He laughed.

The day before, he'd been resting on the couch. Now, he was embarking on a quest to discover his true identity, a beautiful woman at his side. "What a difference a day makes."

She understood completely.

Whatever vibes they had going together felt wonderful. Common sense and good feelings told them that much. Daisy didn't believe in overrationalizing. When life was good it was good.

She grinned back. "Yeah."

Ten

After a dinner of fried chicken, corn bread, and black-eyed peas, Daisy returned to the back porch with John Doe. It was eight P.M. The night was quiet, the scent of roses strong in the air. They sat in a matching pair of wooden rocking chairs. On a table between them, a citronella candle burned.

Daisy cracked her knuckles. It was time to get serious.

"Okay, John Doe. Let's start with the suspicion we have that you're in law enforcement somehow. Let's say that from the state of your clothes and lack of anything official, you're not with city, county, or state police. Let's say, for the sake of a starting point, that you are a detective of some sort. What do you think a detective does?"

"He wears regular clothes to fit the occasion."

In the dark, Daisy beamed at him. "Good start. You were found at night. You were dressed in casual clothes. That means you wanted to blend in with the town and with the dark hours. What else do you think?"

"Detectives hunt for clues that solve cases ranging from theft to murder to missing persons. If I was doing something like that, I might have been wearing casual clothes. We can't focus on anything specific like that. For all we know, I could have been a tourist. This is a tourist town."

"I agree," she admitted. "To tell you the truth, I don't know where to go besides the police for clues."

He understood where she was headed with her thinking. "Spud's commentary today let us know what the cops have figured out about me so far, which is squat. We need to talk to the women who fired up the gossip in town."

Daisy grimaced. She knew her friends quite well. "That would be the entire garden club."

"No. Only Zenith's contribution to start with. Zenith talked to her mother who talked to her friend, a Miss Myrtle I believe, who saw me at the fast food drive-in. I want to quiz the woman who saw me."

Daisy liked talking things over with John Doe. It was like knocking a tennis ball back and forth over a net in a match between two players with equal skill. He anticipated what she might say, then returned with an excellent addition to the conversation.

She enjoyed a man who liked to talk as much as she did. "Good idea."

"I went over the crime scene and found nothing to go on."

"What crime scene?" Her question stopped the flow of their conversation like a tennis ball striking the net.

"The compost pile," he prodded.

"Ohhhh," she said, realizing she had a lot to learn about mystery solving. She only considered the term "crime scene" as something said on TV. "Well, if that's the case, then it's not true we didn't find anything."

"What do you mean?" Another tennis ball in the net.

"It means that you were found in the compost pile. *You* are a body of evidence."

She'd seen enough cop shows to pick up some mystery-solving lingo now that the idea was in her mind. She was having a great time with John Doe and she didn't care if he knew about it.

Daisy didn't believe in keeping her feelings a secret. In her mind, secret-keeping was as big a time-waster as holding a grudge.

"Put that way," he said, "you're right."

She continued her train of investigative thought. "We already took you to the hospital. It was a stroke of good luck to have Dr. Randal on duty. She's sharp."

He understood Daisy completely. "She's a scientist. The facts she discovered about my body and state of mind are objective forms of physical evidence."

John Doe felt in the dark for Daisy's hand. They locked fingers together. He said, "I'm glad she was on duty, too."

Daisy enjoyed the feel of his warm hand against her own. His hand was rough, but not so rough his skin scratched her skin. Daisy wanted to talk the night away. Somehow, she and Chester always ended up arguing. She hadn't realized that until now.

She was also beginning to realize there was a lot about Chester she didn't care to deal with. She had simply put up with him because he was an excellent employee on the one hand, a reliable friend on the other.

Now she wondered if he had been truly sincere about their friendship. Had his behavior been a sophisticated act to get into her pants? She hadn't thought a true friend would cause so many problems when she needed his help, but Chester was causing one problem after another.

Somehow she just couldn't picture John Doe leaving her to deal with an amnesia victim on her own, even if she insisted.

The best thing Daisy could see happening out of the entire drama was to be sure John Doe found out his true identity as quickly as possible. If Chester couldn't understand that, then so be it. "I know one thing we can do, John Doe."

"What?"

"We can go to the police station tomorrow and get Spud to run your fingerprints. If you were in law enforcement, even as a bail bondsman or a parole officer, you would have fingerprints on file."

"Impressive, Daisy."

"Thank you." She cocked her head to the side. "The more I think about it, I really can see you as some sort of PI."

"Don't fit me into a mold," he countered, his tone full of caution. "I could turn out to be a car salesman."

"I'm serious."

"So am I, Daisy."

"What would be the lure of being a PI?" she asked.

He was silent a moment, listening to insects flying in the dark. Thanks to Daisy's citronella candle, none of the bugs landed in the quiet of their rocking chair space. John Doe hadn't felt this good all day. "Most PIs are probably self-employed."

"I bet they travel a lot, too."

"Probably."

Daisy stopped rocking. She turned to gaze at John Doe, but couldn't see his features clearly. The effect was startling. Even in the dark, battered and bruised as he was, missing memory and all, he was the most thrilling man she had ever met.

Forty-eight hours ago she'd been in her bed dreaming about winning a classic rose competition in Tulsa, Oklahoma. Now she was holding hands in the dark with a man she kept thinking of kissing.

She enjoyed gentle kisses out of the blue, kisses like the kind he had given her near the grandiflora roses that afternoon. "So, aside from your missing ID and your missing car, you might have missing luggage."

"I might. I might also be a guy from Oklahoma City or Tulsa trailing after some guy claiming he has a back injury just to get workman's comp."

The idea had merit, but she didn't entertain it for long. "You might. But somebody committing insurance fraud isn't likely to beat you up and leave you for dead."

"Depends on how much money is involved."

"Well, I'm thinking of V.I. Warshawski."

Another ball in the net. "V who?"

"Mystery writer Sara Paretsky has a character named V.I. Warshawski who investigates financial crimes. V.I. travels, kicks butt, and deals with fraud in the course of solving a mystery. Her mystery usually involves murder with money as a motive."

John Doe stifled a groan. First she was talking about TV and now she was talking about books. She definitely thought their experience together was a great adventure. He found her talk of murder chilling.

"This is real life, Daisy."

"I know, but I wanted to point out that insurance fraud could be a reason for murder. Those are the kinds of cases that Sue Grafton's character, Kinsey Millhone, worked on. The Kinsey character worked on a little of this and a little of that. You strike me as that kind of investigator."

Her brain was so on-target she scared him a little. She

was right. He did know too much about investigating crime not to be involved in some capacity with law, either as an enforcer or as an observer.

Either way, the chance of Spud Gurber finding records on him by running his fingerprints through a police computer database was high.

"The problem, Daisy, is that I need to have an identity in order to access driving records and court documents. Since I don't have an identity, I will rely heavily on the observations of the people around me, beginning with you."

"Me?"

"Yes."

He blew out the candle. In the dark, he stood, then pulled her close to him. Six inches of space was between them. He concentrated on the scents of the night. He smelled the smoke from the burning wick.

He savored the aroma of the roses, those wonderful gifts to the human senses Daisy had planted strategically about her home, a unique and restful asylum of color, scent, and privacy which enabled John Doe to maximize his pleasure in Daisy's company.

Near the porch steps, he smelled the pink-lemonade honeysuckle vine she had planted before work that morning. He also inhaled the fragrance of her lovely brown body. "What perfume to do you wear?"

"Elige. It's made by Mary Kay."

Without moving his hands or his feet, John Doe angled his nose toward her right ear. He breathed again. "Elige. It's soft and warm. Like you."

She drew a deep breath, then expelled the air in a rush.

She also took one step back. "Are you sure you have amnesia?"

His tone showed he was puzzled by her question. "About some things, yes. Why do you ask?" He remembered how to dress, how to eat, social etiquette.

"Because if you don't have amnesia," she continued, "if you're working me to get to something I've got, I promise you this, John Doe: I promise I will find out if you've been lying to me all this time. If I find out you've been lying to me, you won't have to worry about Chester breaking your legs. I'll break them myself."

Cutie Pie growled.

The German shepherd stood on the ground beneath the porch steps. She was confident, her body regal and poised by design. There was nothing hostile in her stance, but there was an air of objectivity about her that let John Doe know that even though he had scratched her belly and snuck her dog biscuits when Daisy wasn't looking, Cutie Pie would punch holes in him with her teeth without thinking twice if she thought Daisy was in danger.

John Doe had studied Cutie Pie well enough to understand that she was a working dog. That meant she had a long, smooth stride that covered a lot of ground using very few steps. He also knew she was powerful enough to clear the three porch steps in one leap to knock him down.

Once she had him on his back, he would be at her mercy. He didn't want to be at Cutie Pie's mercy. Her single growl had been short, deep, and deadly.

John Doe slowed his breath. He only blinked when he had to blink. He forced his muscles to relax. His tone was calm, low. "You knew Cutie Pie was here the whole time, didn't you?"

Daisy's laugh wasn't exactly nice.

The sound of her laugh held irony as well as scorn. She seldom felt such a combination of feelings, but at that moment, she wondered how John Doe could think she was so naïve she would accept his word alone that she was safe with him.

Men, she thought, disgusted.

Sometimes she thought men were way too arrogant, especially the big, brawny ones like Chester and John Doe. They were the kind of men who knew they were tough enough to take a licking and still get up swinging.

In their arrogance, Chester and John Doe assumed that because she was small and female and willing to accept people at face value, she needed male protection. This was the first time since meeting John Doe that he had disappointed her.

How did he know she wasn't trained in self-defense? He didn't. How did he know she didn't have a small knife or a tiny, deadly gun in her pocket? He assumed that because she was nice, she was also naïve.

Men, she thought again. Ha!

"Of course I knew Cutie Pie was nearby," she said. "Did you really think I'd sit in the dark all night without a weapon?"

"I thought you trusted me." There was a hint of accusation in his voice.

"I trust the man I know as John Doe," she clarified. "It's the part of you I don't know about that I'm leery of." She took another step back. "Just so you know it, Cutie Pie is never far away."

"Where was she the night I was dumped in your garden?" The hint of accusation was gone from his voice, replaced now with a note of censure.

"She wasn't far away. Every now and then, she sleeps hard."

"That's not a good watchdog."

"She's a country dog. The country is a noisy place. Sometimes the tree frogs get so loud, it's hard to think outside. Trust me. The guys who dumped you out here weren't trying to be heard. Trust me on this, too. Had I screamed then or if I scream now, Cutie Pie would cut your throat with her teeth. Don't ever take me for granted, John Doe. I'm a country girl. Like Cutie Pie, I know when to keep my cool and when to blow my top."

John Doe looked down into Daisy's face in admiration. Her inner strength appealed to his own natural strength. Her independence added weight to her opinions. Her open mind made her approachable. Her approachability and physical allure drew him to her on all mental and emotional levels.

He had assumed she was too trusting and had been wrong. No wonder her mother wasn't breaking down the door to get to her. He noticed that the women had spoken on the phone twice since his arrival to touch base.

Like Cutie Pie, Daisy's mother apparently trusted her daughter's judgment without question. Daisy was a full-package woman. He finally said, "I understand."

"Good," she said, all business. "Now that you finally understand I'm not stupid, let's go inside."

At the kitchen table, he joined her with a pen and a fresh sheet of paper. He put her name at the top of the paper. Then he started asking questions that led to the answers he put on the paper.

Daisy Rogers

Age: 35
Single
No children
Runs a rose nursery and garden shop
Five feet three inches tall
120 lbs
Shoulder-length brown hair
Ginger colored skin
Dark brown colored eyes
Casual dresser
Excellent southern-style cook and veteran gardener
Key interesting fact: Good Samaritan

She took the paper and pen from him and treated him the same way he had treated her. "My turn."

John Doe

Six feet two inches tall
200 lbs
Ebony colored skin
Light brown eyes
Casual dresser
Excellent thinker
Organized
Observant
Attentive
Key interesting fact: amnesia victim

"You're good, Daisy."

Her expression was somber. This guy was way more than a handsome face. He wanted to know as much about her as she did about him. "And you're so terrific at profiling, I'm getting suspicious of you myself."

She pushed their papers aside. "I'm gonna make us some chamomile."

"I'll get the cups. That stuff is pretty relaxing. It says 'Sleepytime' on the box, but it's more soothing than sleep-inducing."

"That's why I like it."

While the kettle boiled water, John Doe picked up their conversation where they had left off. "What do you know about profiling?"

"Everything I learned about profiling I learned on TV. But what you're doing is different. You're breaking profiling down item by item like you know what you're doing. I just have a general picture. I think you had to have been into some sort of law enforcement."

"Maybe."

"Uh-uh. I'm serious. I don't think you were a city cop like Spud or even a county cop. I see you as some sort of agency cop."

"The FBI?"

"I don't know. Something like that. Maybe even a PI like we talked about. A bounty hunter even. You were dressed so casual when I found you that I'd be surprised if you were with any law force that requires a uniform. From state police to city police, there would be national coverage if you went down."

"I agree. I'd also be driving an official car, and none was found."

She poured water from the kettle into huge stoneware mugs with roosters on them. "You could have been off duty."

"True. But as an official of the law, I'd still be hunted for across the state via public broadcast."

"You wouldn't if you were with the government," Daisy reasoned.

"Depends on what kind of branch within the government system. There's more than the FBI and the CIA. There's the U.S. Marshals Service, Immigration, and the Postal Inspection Service—"

She studied him over the rim of her rooster mug. "Wait a minute. I don't think even Spud would have come up with the Postal Inspection Service. I mean, I just can't picture Spud Gurber worrying about mail fraud." She paused. "I don't think you were a random victim, John Doe. You know too much about the law."

"I realized that myself after talking to you."

She nodded her head in agreement. "Spud sure corrected his attitude when you came around. I don't blame him. Your body language and demeanor shout authority. I bet we find prints on you. I know Spud went fishing this weekend. He'll be back in the saddle on Monday. We don't have to wait until Monday, but it would give you a little more time to rest up if we do. I asked him about it on the phone."

"Another day won't hurt. Anyway, I was glad to see Spud do it. Shape up that is. It means there are good cops in the Guthrie Police Department. The worse thing a police force can have is a group of men and women running around with badges and no conscience. Spud has a conscience."

"He does."

"Chester is a different problem."

Daisy frowned. "You mean his jealousy?"

"Yeah."

"Don't worry," she scoffed. "I can handle Chester."

John Doe took a sip of tea. He'd handle Chester himself.

Eleven

It was early Monday morning, almost two hours before the garden shop opened for business. Daisy and John Doe shared a breakfast of cinnamon raisin bagels smothered in classic Philadelphia Cream Cheese.

To go with the bagels, there was coffee, purchased from D.G.'s at 301 South Division, Daisy's favorite coffee shop. The flavor of coffee they savored together was toasted almond.

Feeling rested, able to move with more comfort than pain, John Doe was ready to tackle the business of repaying his hostess for her trademark kindness. "Okay, Daisy. I need to earn my keep around your place."

She nodded her head in assent. Dressed in his original sweats, his attitude upbeat and friendly, Daisy understood his signal that they were moving into new territory together in their relationship.

It was time for the giving to be returned.

"Sounds good to me," she said. For the moment, she'd forgotten about Chester. Chester wouldn't like knowing John Doe was officially up and about.

Daisy was quickly discovering that John Doe was handy to have around. On Sunday, he had done some minor repairs around the house while she took care of the business books for the week.

He had fixed the silverware drawer that was broken in the kitchen and replaced the screen on the front door with the new one she had bought several weeks before. He had even mowed the lawn using the lawn tractor.

When questioned about his activities, he'd claimed that the silverware drawer was a no-brainer to repair, the screen door had forced him to stretch through the soreness of his body, and riding the lawn tractor had given him plenty of time to think.

The fact that Chester realized John Doe was handy for Daisy to have around prompted him to do whatever he could to discredit John Doe. He failed miserably, instead lowering Daisy's good opinion of him. Nothing Chester said or did stopped Daisy's growing admiration for her mysterious guest.

This failure on Chester's part to cause a rift added to the tension each person felt over John Doe's identity crisis. Chester hadn't liked hearing that she needed him to open the garden shop while she and John Doe went to see Spud about fingerprints. Chester would have preferred to close the garden shop so all three of them could visit Spud at the Guthrie Police Station. Chester was behaving like a jilted suitor instead of an employee.

Chester kept a foot on Daisy's nerves.

In contrast, John Doe kept getting under her skin. Her positive feelings continued on their way to the police department. It was a short drive.

"What would you like to do?" she asked him as they drove back to the garden shop after Spud arranged for the fingerprinting. It had taken them an hour to answer a few questions and to leave a set of John Doe's prints.

John Doe was quiet for a moment. "My being inside the garden shop will cause too much of a stir among your customers. Besides, when I'm in there, I feel like I'm on exhibition or something. Also, I don't know squat about gardening. I've never had a plant. Not even a fake one."

Daisy had to admit he didn't look like a plant-nurturing person. She thought it was a good idea to talk to plants, something she did whenever she watered them. She couldn't imagine John Doe talking to a plant. "How do you know you've never had a plant or that you don't know squat about gardening?"

He scratched his head. "I must know in the same way I still remember how to walk and talk. I just know."

She laughed at his consternation. It had to be weird to remember simple details about his life but nothing strong enough to identify himself. "I'll accept that. So, where do you want to start?"

John Doe took his time coming up with an answer. "Since you specialize in roses, I suppose I'd like to know why. The way you tend them all the time, they seem kind of temperamental."

She laughed. "Good observation. You're right. First time rose gardeners are often surprised to find out they can't just stick their new roses in the ground and water them the way they can with many shrubs like azaleas or boxwood or privet."

He enjoyed her enthusiasm about her gardening hobby/business. For a moment, he wished he shared her passion.

He bet if she had amnesia, she would still have a love

for gardening. For her, it was as natural as eating or drinking, habits he remembered even though he didn't know his own home address.

"I don't have a clue what you're talking about," he admitted.

She waved him off and kept going. "Rose gardening is like any other gardening, which is to say that it's mostly a trial-and-error situation. Plant health, proper feeding and watering schedules, as well as weather conditions, hold a lot of importance in growing a beautiful garden."

Staring intently out the window, John Doe hoped to trigger his memory by seeing something familiar. He didn't. That he couldn't remember why he was in Guthrie drove him crazy. Listening to Daisy calmed his nerves.

She pulled her 1994 black Chevy Tahoe into the driveway of her bungalow-style home. Still, Daisy kept her commentary running about gardening. Perhaps she was nervous. Perhaps she sensed his melancholy about his memory loss and sought to distract him.

They both knew he couldn't learn about gardening with a crash course, but the overview she provided was helpful. She said, "On the one hand, roses need pampering. On the other hand, fossils have been found of roses that date back to more than thirty million years. They couldn't have been pampered back then, yet they survived."

John Doe left the sport utility and walked around to meet Daisy. She was already out of the car. He said, "So they started out wild."

"Most plants do. Anyway, roses first turned up in Asia and can be found in such seemingly odd places as Alaska, Siberia, and even Africa. Crazy as it sounds, some roses will grow even in sand."

"I can't picture a rosebush in the sand."

"True wild roses don't look like the kind you find at the florist or even in my garden shop. For the most part, wild roses have a single layer of five petals that look a lot like apple blossoms."

John Doe stared at Daisy with a fresh eye.

On her head was a straw hat with a leather drawstring. She wore a black mock turtleneck with no sleeves, faded jeans, and green rubber gardening clogs. As usual, she didn't wear any makeup. Her skin was flawless. She looked wonderful.

"How did you get into this field?" he asked. They stopped at the porch steps.

"My mom. She specializes in cottage gardening and old roses. I got the bug from her. In fact, it was my mom who suggested I open a garden shop. When her arthritis made it difficult to work in her garden, I took over. I got into experimenting."

"Experimenting with what?"

"I wanted to grow a rose that was just for my mom, something that had never existed and that no one else in the world would have."

He never expected a response like that one. Daisy was full of surprises. The more time he spent with her, the more time he wanted to spend. There was something old and new about her at the same time.

She was wise like an old person because she didn't rattle easy, but new because he had never met her before, had never experienced the freshness of her ideas; at least he didn't feel as if he had.

He hoped they could be friends after his identity crisis

was resolved. A future without Daisy suddenly seemed dim. "Did you design one?"

"Yes." They left the porch steps and went into the house. Daisy threw her purse on a small scratched table by the front door. He followed her into the kitchen, where she washed her hands and set to work making coffee.

"Where is the rose you designed?"

She smiled. "In my mother's garden. When I was a kid, I thought everything grew in my mother's garden. When I became a teen, I realized that wasn't true. The rose I made grows only in my mother's yard. Nowhere else."

He bowed from the waist. "Wow."

She curtsied. "I'll take you there sometime."

"I'm looking forward to it."

They sat in silence for a while. Sunlight poured through the windows. The kitchen was clean. The refrigerator hummed. The coffee dripped. The scene was perfect, mellow.

"I love your place," he said without thinking.

"Me too."

"Have you ever thought of leaving Guthrie?"

"Not seriously. I've traveled, but whenever I come back home, I'm always so thankful for the quiet. I like not dealing with traffic jams and impatient crowds. There's no place in the world like Guthrie. When it's hot outside, I fool around in my garden and pretend like the heat of summer is burning my stress away."

He laughed. "What?"

She explained. "A sauna can be wet. It can be dry. I like the dry heat. Dry heat burns the stress from my muscles and makes them relax on their bones. After a day in the sun like that, I feel as if I've had a pleasant workout.

Then I shower and sit on the back porch and enjoy all the flowers I've planted in my garden. This is paradise, John Doe. Everything I want in life is right at my own front door."

On impulse, he kissed her cheek. "I feel rested here. I think before I came to Guthrie, I was tired, Daisy. I'm really lucky you let me stay. I can never thank you enough for what you've done for me."

"You're welcome."

John Doe served them black coffee in the rooster mugs. He doubted he would ever see a rooster dish again without thinking of Daisy Rogers. "I know you've got to get back to work soon."

She sighed. "True."

"You seem to keep a steady flow of customer traffic here."

Her pride was evident. Her skin and eyes glowed with good feeling. "I do. The location for the garden shop is excellent. It's right on the way home for the residents and right on the way out of town for the tourists. It's probably why my garden was the perfect place for the . . . uh . . . villains . . . to dump your body."

"Quick way in. Quick way out."

"Yep. But to answer your question: The nursery thrives because gardeners everywhere can't resist a haven made especially for them. Many people I meet think the Chinese had the first formal nurseries. Those same people are surprised to discover that Egyptians grew roses in nurseries for the Romans."

"Egyptians crossed the Mediterranean with roses?" There was wonder in John Doe's eyes when he looked at her. She was definitely more than a pretty young face.

"Ah, so you know your world geography." She raised her rooster mug in a toast. The clink of their ceramic mugs was soft. "We can add that to your list of attributes. The answer to your question is yes."

She downed the last of her coffee, then finished off the pot by pouring the last of the dark brew into their mugs. The taste was rich and strong the way she liked it, Seattle's Best from D.G.'s.

She said, "Not only did the Egyptians get live roses across the Mediterranean, the secret to how they did it successfully is still a mystery. What the Egyptians did was remarkable. It's a long trip by those old-time boats. Like you said, roses need lots of care."

"Except wild roses."

"Yes. Wild roses survive because they have to compete for nourishment with other wild things. It's the classic case of survival of the fittest. It's how a rose can thrive in the subzero climate of Alaska and the dry sands of New England shores. Would it surprise you to know I think of you as a wild rose?"

He smiled. His teeth were white and well shaped. "Because I sprouted in the compost pile?"

"Not only that, John Doe. Like something wild, you have thrived. Like a single row of wild rose petals, you have a single layer of simplicity."

He raised a brow in mild surprise. "You think I'm simple?"

"No. I'm referring to the fact that you are a healthy man with amnesia. That's simple. But despite your amnesia, you have found a way to thrive in a hostile environment."

"You aren't hostile."

"The situation is hostile. Chester is a perfect example. He hates your guts because he's threatened by what he doesn't know about you."

"He doesn't think I'll hurt you. If he did, he'd never leave you alone with me. No man who called himself your friend would let you fend for yourself."

"It's the only reason I'm putting up with his bad behavior. But to tell you the truth, I'll never feel the same way about Chester again. I'm not into rough stuff. I don't care for unnecessary violence. That's all he seems to be able to think about—breaking your legs and anything else he can get away with. That's macho bull crap."

"It's human nature."

"Ha! Give me a rose any day of the week. In my experience, roses need less pampering than the male ego."

"Ouch."

"Let's go outside. I've got thirty minutes left before I take over the shop. I want to show you something."

They rinsed their mugs and left them in the sink.

Outside, she pushed him over to a corner of fruit-bearing plants. "What do you think these plants have in common?"

He read the tags. "Raspberry, strawberry. You can eat them."

"You can eat roses, too."

"No."

"Yes. On a rose, after all the petals drop off, a round ball called a hip is left behind. Besides being full of vitamin C, the inside of a hip is loaded with seeds. The whole thing is edible."

"You're kidding."

She lifted her face to him and smiled, unaware she made

his heart race in appreciation. Her company did wonders for John Doe's soul.

"In England," she said, "a favorite specialty dish among gardeners is rose-hip jelly. It's served with scones. Anyway, roses, raspberries, and strawberries are in the same genus of plants called *Rosa.*"

He felt a flash of pain across his forehead. With it came a brief wave of nausea. He felt dizzy. "That name."

"Rosa?"

"Yes." He frowned in concentration as he tried to put a face with the name. "I know someone by that name. I can almost see who it is."

He ran a hand around the back of his neck.

"This is frustrating, Daisy. I've got to find out who I am. I refuse to let things go on this way."

"Rosa must be pretty important if just the sound of her name can make you grab your neck like that." She pointed to a three-legged wood stool painted red. Throughout the garden, there were chairs and benches, impromptu resting spots for the visitors to enjoy. "Sit down."

He sat. The last thing he wanted to do was embarrass himself by passing out at a pretty woman's feet. "I know what you're doing, Daisy. Thank you."

"What am I doing?"

"On the surface, you're rambling, but in truth, you're relaxing me so that my subconscious can work."

"You're a deep fellow, John Doe."

"And you're a remarkable woman."

"Thank you. Enough about me. How's your head?"

"Better."

"Good." She handed him a rake and pointed her thumb in the direction of three boxes of pure funk.

"No."

"If you don't do it, I will."

"I'll do it."

"Good. The smell ought to take your mind off your head. Maybe it will get your subconscious on the topic of Rosa and you'll get the answer you need."

He snapped the fingers of his right hand to his head in military salute. "Aye-aye, sir." He clicked his heels. "Right away, sir."

She smacked his arm. She liked his sense of humor. "I'll see you in a couple of hours for lunch."

"What are we having?"

"Scones with rose-hip tea."

After she left, he peered into the brown packing boxes of pure funk. The funk was the stink of well-rotted cow manure. He spread it around a set of hybrid teas called Confidence, Candy Stripe, and Command Performance.

Someone else had fertilized the A and B sections of the hybrid teas. He figured it was Chester.

As he worked in the soil of the C section, John Doe felt the pain in his head subside. No wonder Daisy was always at peace with herself. Gardening was like food to the spirit. John Doe set to work with a whistle. His mind was clear, his step light, his spirit filled with well-being.

He owed his sense of pleasure and peace to Daisy, his very own special rose. Whatever would he do without her, now that she had come into his life? At some point, his memory would return.

When it did, when his present was reconnected with his past, where would Daisy fit into his future?

The questions were endless. Not wanting to let go of his gardening euphoria, John Doe relaxed his mind by concentrating on the repetitive cycle of lifting, bending, and spreading the cow manure in Daisy's garden.

By the time her ulterior motive dawned on him, John Doe had spread two bags of manure. She wanted him to remember that from the stink of rotten manure came beauty, the roses in her garden.

Having him spread manure was Daisy's way of making lemonade out of lemons.

John Doe didn't just smile, he laughed outright.

Twelve

After the garden shop closed that night, the couple was ready to do some legwork into the mystery of John Doe's identity. Chester had gone home, angry because he wasn't invited to tag along.

John Doe spoke to Daisy. "All that talk about being partners was fine until the time for action came up. Going to the police station this morning was one thing. Going into other people's homes to ask questions is something else. That something else is an uncontrolled environment. Anything can go wrong under those conditions. With that in mind, I don't want you to go."

Daisy had sunglasses, a straw gardening hat, a big purse, and a huge smile on her face. They were on their way to her sport utility truck.

"It's too late to back out now, John Doe. Besides, Zenith's mother will never let you into the house by yourself. You need me to open doors around Guthrie. Don't forget, we're a small town."

He opened the driver's door for her. Once she was inside, he leaned on the door frame. He talked to her through the open window. "I thought good old Southern hospitality was all I'd need to open doors around here."

She smiled. "That's fiction. In real life, citizens in small

Southern towns open their doors for a stranger when he can prove his connection to somebody in town that the citizen knows. Zenith's mother doesn't have to know you to let you into her house. She has to know me."

He chuckled.

"Anyway," she said, "there's no reason for you to worry about my safety, because I'll be with you."

She cranked up the truck.

"Point taken." He squeezed her arm. "Daisy?"

"Yes?"

"Since everybody knows you, especially Zenith's mother, I don't think you need camouflage."

"It's the dark glasses, huh?" She flipped down the driver's-side visor so she could study her reflection in the mirror attached to the back of it. "I kind of thought they were over the top when I put them on. I don't usually wear them. I'll lose the glasses so Zenith's mother can see my eyes."

"Great idea. And Daisy?"

"Yep?"

John Doe ran his hand down her shoulder bone until he was able to cup her bicep. Her flesh felt young and supple and wonderful. He leaned his head through the window, pulled her to his face, then slowly, slowly, his eyes gazing into hers, met her lips with his own.

Their kiss stole his own breath away.

The gesture was so perfect, Daisy thought she might melt in her seat. The kisses themselves weren't spectacular. It was the way he approached her that she liked. As big and tough as he was, John Doe took the time to be gentle. She appreciated that fact.

"You are the best when it comes to kissing."

He was laughing before he opened his eyes. "You're a little bit like Tammy from that old movie, *Tammy and the Bachelor.*"

"Naïve?"

"Loving." He traced her chin with his finger. "Before long I won't want to leave here at all."

"Don't."

He looked away from her. In the distance, squirrels chased each other through the cottonwood trees. "That wouldn't be fair to either of us."

She held her breath for an instant. "We better get going. Make this investigation real."

He strode to the passenger side of the car, climbed inside, and buckled up before looking at her again. He felt like pulling her over the seat onto his lap.

She said, "It's good to have someone to bounce ideas off of, so the way I see it, John Doe, you need me to cover your back so nobody sneaks up on you again. I'll do for you what Cutie Pie does for me."

As he was sure she intended, her statement changed the entire atmosphere between them.

"What are you talking about?" he asked.

She waited a beat before she answered. "I figure the only way somebody could have laid you out the way you were laid out is if you'd been ambushed. You're too observant not to see you were about to get clobbered."

His voice hardened to steel. "This isn't a game. It's not TV."

She was adamant. "I don't give a hoot about TV. By now you ought to know that. I do what feels right to me. Going after the bad guys feels right." Cool confidence laced her voice. Good or bad, right or wrong, Daisy had no problem making a decision.

John Doe didn't have to know her as long as Chester did to figure she wasn't bluffing. "Okay. What can you bring to the table?"

His response caught her off guard. But then, she realized, if it was true that John Doe was still in trouble, it was also true that whoever beat him up knew he wasn't dead and that sooner or later he would turn up again to finish whatever had been started.

She and John Doe couldn't afford to argue.

"You mean right now for the investigation?"

He winced at the excited tone in her voice. Too much excitement in a potentially volatile situation was dangerous. He kept his voice controlled. It carried no hint of the worry he felt about Daisy's safety. But he was definitely worried.

He could just see her charging to his defense in a tricky moment. He could see her getting hurt as she tried to keep him safe. He didn't need to be kept safe—she did.

Looking at her flushed face, listening to her excited voice, he understood that the best way to keep Daisy safe was to keep her at his side. "Of course."

"Maybe we ought to call a TV news station," she said. "If the public knew what was going on, maybe someone would recognize you and could help, maybe . . ."

The steel in John Doe's voice got harder. "Trust me. A television interview would be too risky."

"I've got to trust you or else this thing won't work. For a fact, I don't know what I'm doing, but you sure seem to have a handle on things."

"So I noticed." He looked disgruntled.

Daisy jumped full out into her adventure with the new man in her life. Like the film character John Shaft in the movie *Shaft*, John Doe was a complicated man, a man only his woman could understand.

Since he had no definite memories about his identity and since he wore no wedding ring, Daisy figured she was the number-one woman in John Doe's life. Even if he wasn't a complicated man, events surrounding his life were certainly complicated.

Much to her growing delight Daisy was caught in the middle of a drama that had the potential to make or break the rest of a man's life. Her life had been easy until John Doe turned up.

Whatever happened, the entire experience was simply wonderful.

Right then, Daisy decided she would enjoy her adventure as it happened. She would deal with whatever consequences came her way and take the end results of her actions without complaining.

She could handle it.

She was not like Tammy in *Tammy and the Bachelor*. She was a grown woman with a solid life of her own. She was not a little girl looking for somebody to take care of her. As the saying went, big girls don't cry. Neither did Daisy.

If she got hurt, either emotionally or physically, it would be her own fault. John Doe and Chester kept reminding her of danger.

They were worried about how they would feel if something bad happened to her. She was accountable because she insisted on staying neck-deep in the action.

Action.

The word caused her to focus intently on John Doe. "The closer we get to some live action in this thing, the more you behave as if you're an authority on missing people."

"Yeah. I noticed that, too."

John Doe opened the writing tablet he carried in his pocket. Daisy had given him the tablet to carry around in case he remembered some detail about his past that might be important to solving his identity.

He clicked the point of a pen into place. "No physical evidence was left at the crime scene that would incriminate anybody in particular. The way I showed up without ID and transportation is enough evidence to conclude there is foul play."

"Makes sense," she agreed.

"I find it hard to believe I was abducted from somewhere and left alive. I doubt I was ambushed for the same reason. But perhaps I went to a meeting somewhere, a meeting that somehow went wrong."

"Any ideas about who or what or where?"

"Not really. Mostly just bits and pieces. It's a reason why I want to write things down as we go along. I'm hoping that at some point, I'll notice a connection between where I disappeared from and where I am now."

"Do you honestly believe you can do what the regular cops can't or won't do?"

His response was quick and decisive. "Yes."

"Why?"

"I'm my only case."

"What do you expect from me?"

John Doe admired her confidence, the wholehearted way she tackled the problem in front of her. "Always remember we're in this thing together. For all the calm we're experiencing right now, this whole situation could blow up in our faces. An unknown enemy is the most dangerous enemy of all."

"I know."

"And Daisy?"

Her breath caught. "Yes?"

"I may not be as innocent as you think."

Zenith's mother opened the door before Daisy could knock.

"Get in here, girl. It's hot. Damn hot." The older woman ushered the couple into her A-frame house.

"Thank you for seeing us, Mrs. . . . ?"

"John Doe," the older woman said, "you don't have to be so formal. You can call me Miss Tilly the same way Daisy does."

"Okay, Miss Tilly."

Miss Tilly adjusted her Diana Ross and the Supremes–style wig, retro 1966. She was six feet tall, round from face to ankle, her skin a mottled mixture of brown with patches of white. She wore a light blue cotton dress, no stockings, and penny loafers.

She eyed him with the practiced gaze of a college dorm mother. "You look like a man who needs steak and eggs for breakfast. Hold on while I fix you a plate of fried pork chops and collard greens."

"No ma'am—I mean, no thank you, Miss Tilly."

"Some cornbread, too. It'll only take a minute."

John Doe raised a hand to stop her. "Miss Tilly, that's all right. I don't need anything. Honest."

Miss Tilly didn't hear him. She was already on her way to the kitchen.

Daisy grinned. "Now you know why we only had scones for lunch. Nobody leaves Miss Tilly's house without eating something. She doesn't believe in crackers with cheese on top or a simple glass of iced tea. When company comes calling at Miss Tilly's, they can expect to eat something solid, even if it's just chicken wings."

"You're kidding."

"Just wait until we get to Miss Myrtle's."

He groaned.

She laughed outright. "Oh, Miss Myrtle won't stuff you with dinner food. She'll stuff you with dessert. Her cobblers are legendary."

"I love a good cobbler. Will it be peach?"

"Probably."

Daisy stashed her purse on the floor next to the plastic-covered chair she sat on. The entire living room set was covered in clear plastic. The furniture underneath was red. "Miss Myrtle uses the fruit from the trees in her yard to make her pies."

"My mouth is watering."

"Don't let Miss Tilly hear you say your mouth is watering for Miss Myrtle's food," Daisy warned.

"I thought you said they're friends."

She laughed. "Best friends make the best enemies. They know all the dirt on each other."

"Excellent observation, Daisy. I wonder if the person who arranged for me to be roughed up is a best friend turned enemy?"

"You think that because you're still alive?"

Miss Tilly returned with platters of food in time to hear

the last two statements. "I know it is. The two fellas he was with before he went to Sonic for cheddar peppers were nothing but trouble. It's the lady who treated him like he was her own personal property who makes sense about a friend being his enemy."

"The lady?" The couple said together.

Miss Tilly's grin was sly. She wanted to drag her ten minutes of fame out. She had never been involved in a missing persons case. She patted her Diana Ross retro wig to make sure it was still in place. "Boy, how's those fried pork chops?"

He knew a stalling tactic when he saw one. "Dynamite."

"And the greens?" she asked.

"Fresh, right?"

"Picked 'em myself."

Eventually, Miss Tilly settled down for some serious conversation. "Let me tell you what I saw."

John Doe continued to stuff his face with delicious food, but nodded his head in assent that she should begin. She needed no further prompting. "The first thing I saw was you, and you were eating your lunch at Sonic like it was your last meal."

"I wolfed it down?"

"No. You ate slowly as if you had all the time in the world and even if you didn't have all the time in the world you was gonna pretend like you did. Hell. I enjoy seeing a man get the full taste of his food. Those chili peppers are wonderful."

"Not as good as your collard greens."

The older woman preened before him. "Keep those compliments coming, boy. Keep 'em coming."

"Did I have a car?"

"No. You came on foot and left on foot."

"In what direction did I go?"

"You walked north on Division, just past D.G.'s Coffee on the corner of Vilas and Division across from the one-hour photo place."

"Go on," John Doe prodded.

"After that, I lost track of you. I didn't think about you again until Myrtle told me about you being at the garden club meeting on Saturday night. I had heard about the man Daisy found in her garden but I never expected that man to be you. Life is just full of coincidence and surprise ain't it, boy?"

"Yes, ma'am."

"Call me Miss Tilly. Everybody does. Well, not everybody. Some people call me Sister Tilly or Mother Tilly depending on what age is talking to me. How old are you, boy?"

"I figure I'm in my middle thirties. Why?"

"You don't look like a crook. Don't look like a crackhead, either. I'm just wondering what a nice fellow like you is doing in a place like this?"

"Guthrie is a great place from everything I've seen."

"Like any other city, it's got its share of problems."

Miss Tilly offered John Doe more pork chops, which he refused.

"Sometimes," she said, "it seems like Guthrie's problems seem like they're on a bigger scale than in large cities."

"What do you mean?" Daisy asked.

"I mean because we don't have as many people in Guthrie as, say, Tulsa or Oklahoma City or Broken Arrow, whatever does go on takes on a bigger scale. For example, if Myrtle's house burned down, the whole community would be affected. But if a house burned down in a big city, it would hardly bother anybody except the people who live on the same street as the burned house. Are you hearing what I'm saying, boy?"

"I think so," John Doe responded. "You're saying that if something bad happens in this town, the truth will eventually come out and that even though I look like a nice guy, you believe looks can be deceiving."

Miss Tilly nodded her head in approval.

John Doe continued. "That's why you gave the example of big city versus small city. In a big city, there are more recreational activities to do for example, but because there are so many people, those recreational activities carry less punch than they would for a person going from a small city like Guthrie to a big city like Tulsa. The small-town person is most likely to have the largest reaction."

"Sharp boy, Daisy."

Daisy grinned. "Yes, he is."

"But he left out something important," the older woman said.

"What's that?" Daisy asked, shifting forward in her seat.

"You."

"What about me?"

"If something happens to you, it will affect a big chunk of the city because you're known all over the place. In Oklahoma City or Tulsa or Broken Arrow, you'd be one woman in a thousand. Out here, you're one woman in a hundred. And only one woman in this city is named Daisy.

You were born and raised here. So were your people. You belong to us. He don't.'"

John Doe sat a little straighter on the red plastic-covered camel-back sofa. "I better watch my back, is what you're saying?"

Miss Tilly kept a steady gaze on him. "Front and sides, too."

John Doe rose to shake Miss Tilly's hand. "Thank you very much for the dinner. It was great."

"Ain't got to tell me that, but I appreciate hearing it anyway. Shows that your mama raised you right. What's her name, anyway?"

"DeAnn," he replied without thinking first.

Daisy slapped a hand to her mouth. "John Doe!"

He grinned. "Must have been Miss Tilly's food."

"That's right, honey," the older woman said with a wink. "My greens are pure magic."

On the way to Daisy's truck, John Doe pulled her into his arms for a kiss that gave her butterflies. "Thanks, Daisy."

Her eyes flashed with delight. "You're welcome."

Inside the house, Miss Tilly watched John Doe kiss Daisy as if he forgot they were standing on the sidewalk. After they drove away, she sat down on the sofa and picked up the phone from the coffee table.

She called Chester's mother.

Thirteen

It took all Chester's self-control not to slam the phone down in a rage after his mother called him. If it was the last thing he ever did, he was determined to get rid of John Doe. He'd been nothing but trouble since Daisy'd found him in her garden.

Now they were on their way to Miss Myrtle's house. John Doe was going to sit down at Miss Myrtle's dining room table with a big bowl of peach cobbler, vanilla ice cream on top. It was her standard way of treating her guests.

John Doe didn't deserve that kind of favoritism. He deserved to be treated like the outsider he was to Guthrie: seen but not heard.

Chester paid a visit to his partner in crime. Harold Brown's apartment was lean on charm. The walls were dulled from white to dingy gray; the tan carpet was so bare in places, Harold had to hold the ragged edges down with duct tape to keep his guests from tripping.

For Chester, the most interesting article in the musty apartment was Harold himself. Harold was a scrawny strip of human flesh with the biggest gray eyes Chester had ever seen, with long black lashes. The orbs on Harold were popped open in a constant state of surprise, and since his eyes tended to shift from side to side, their roaming effect made him look crazy.

Chester had seen firsthand how people steered clear of his host on the streets of Guthrie when he picked him up from time to time, under the guise of being a Good Samaritan.

Chester would take Harold out to get something to eat, but they were exchanging criminal information.

Harold's oddball look made excellent camouflage. Looking and sometimes acting odd helped him glean all sorts of juicy tidbits to snitch and tell. Few people, Chester had learned from an early age, paid attention to folks they thought were missing a few marbles—people like Harold. Every bit as conniving as Chester, Harold Brown had marbles to spare.

As different as Laurel was to Hardy, the two men made excellent partners in crime.

Chester said, "Tell me what you found out about John Doe."

Harold polished off a malt liquor beer, smacked the bottom of the empty tin can on the gritty dinette table, wiped his damp lips with the back of one ashy black hand, and said, "Don't you want to sit down first?"

"No."

Harold blinked once, shrugged his left shoulder, then headed from the dinette to the living room. It only took him six steps to reach his destination. "Ex-cuse-m-wa if I sit down. I got corns on my baby toes."

Chester pulled a chair from the dinette, flipped it backward, then straddled it, both arms across the top of the chair. "Tell me."

Harold sat on the round ottoman he kept in front of his

sagging old couch. The leather on the ottoman was cracked, its sharp edges held together with the same thick tape as the tape on the floor. "You ain't got to rush me."

"I don't have all night," Chester warned.

Harold chuckled, the sound every bit as nasty as his breath, which smelled of the extra onions he special ordered with the burger he washed down with his beer. "The m-a-n in question is one Kenneth Gunn. He's a retired cop turned private investigator. Heard he's respected but pretty much a loner. No business partner, no old lady, no kiddies. Nothing."

"Interesting."

Greedy little Harold rubbed his ashy hands together. "It gets better."

"Go on."

Harold leaned so far forward he smelled the cherry scent of the Chap Stick slathered all over Chester's lips. Unlike himself, Harold noted, Chester didn't have any ash on him. He was as spit-shined and polished as usual. "Kenneth Gunn killed another cop."

For the first time that evening Chester smiled, the look ugly and feral. "Tell me everything."

Harold cleared his throat. "As you know, I never reveal my sources. I can tell you this. The man you know as John Doe once worked with the Internal Affairs Division in Wichita, Kansas. He was investigating some kind of street scam being run by dirty cops."

"Go on."

"The cops set up a fencing shop disguised as a thrift store. They bought stuff over the counter from small-time thieves, mostly kids and junkies. Those kinds of people ain't likely to know some things they think is fake jewelry is really the gen-u-ine article."

"I see."

Harold took another whiff of cherry-flavored Chap Stick lip balm and thought he might get some, too. "I don't think so. I heard them rogue cops bought a real diamond stick pin for twenty bucks when the damn thing was really worth forty grand. Only instead of turning in the pin like they should've, they kept it and sold it for their own profit. Somehow or another the sale of that pin got 'em some IAD trouble."

Chester selected a toothpick from his pants pocket, stuck the wooden stick between his too-white teeth, and said, "Enter the crooked cop hunter, a.k.a. Kenneth Gunn."

"Uh-huh. The bad cops threw themselves a little party. They invited all the regular thieves to it, but somehow or another things got uh-guh-ly and Gunn killed another cop dead. Kerplewee. That's all she wrote, folks."

"I get it."

Harold straightened his spine. "Of course you get it. That's why you the man." He placed big emphasis on the word *man*.

Chester ignored the quick verbal kiss to his one-hundred-percent-silk-covered behind. "Gunn must have been conning the con men by posing as one of their regular thieves. Was there a shootout?"

"Yes indeedee."

Chester's criminal brain waves were running lickety-split. "And Kenneth Gunn ended up killing one of his own."

"That's how it went down. After he was cleared of wrongdoing by the po-lice department, he quit."

"But," Chester pointed out, "he's still dangerous."

"Could be. Probably is." Harold rubbed his scaly old hands together and grinned, his gray eyes glittering with malicious glee. "So. My man. My brother. Why you wanna know about this dude?"

Chester's toothpick snapped, the small half of it falling to the ground, the big half of it splintered between the teeth at one corner of his mouth. "I've got the feeling Kenneth Gunn's been turning my woman against me. She won't talk to me like she used to, something new since this John Doe character came on the scene."

Harold lifted his butt to one side, broke wind, then waved a hand through the air to fan away the fumes. "You ain't got no woman."

Unwilling to give Harold the satisfaction of seeing his disgust over the crude behavior, Chester canned the urge to shield his nose from the dead-rat fumes he was half convinced might knock him flat.

With all the grace of an aristocrat, he stood, pulled his snakeskin wallet from the same pocket where he kept his toothpicks, tossed some money into Harold Brown's snickering face, and said, "That's what you think. Now I just need to figure out why John Doe, otherwise known as Kenneth Gunn, is in town."

Fourteen

It was the next day, Tuesday, closing time at Daisy's Rose and Garden Shop. Daisy was knee-deep into an argument with Chester. He was sweeping floors. She was restocking supplies not only to clean the place up, but to burn off steam.

She slapped one bag of seeds after another into the seed rack, her efforts more rough than was necessary to get the job done. After breaking down the box the seeds had come in with as much noise as possible, she finally said, "If you hadn't been eavesdropping on my conversation with John Doe, we wouldn't be fighting right now."

"And just when exactly were you going to tell me what was going on?" Chester fired back. He threw the broom against a wall.

Daisy stared at her friend with open disgust. This was their first real fight, and the fight was a doozy. "When I was ready."

"Let's start from the top."

Daisy couldn't believe the high-handed way Chester was talking to her. He talked to her as if he were her significant other with the right to know exactly what she had going on between her and John Doe.

She spoke to Chester out of respect for an increasingly

strained friendship, but there was a whole lot of anger thrown into her attitude. Involving him at the beginning of her adventure with John Doe had been a mistake.

If she hadn't involved Chester in the beginning, she would feel more comfortable now telling him to suck an egg and get out of her business. She couldn't do that; John Doe was his business, too.

"First of all, I think John Doe is somehow connected to the law."

"Why?"

She told him.

Chester's intensity was almost frightening. "I don't like all this mysterious stuff, all this waiting for something to happen."

Daisy was glad the two of them were having it out. She hated being at odds with Chester. He was one of her best friends. "Me either. But that's the way it is."

"This could blow up in your face."

"True."

"Wake up, Daisy. To take on anybody's troubles is tough. This guy's troubles are big-time. You don't need his kind of problems. He could be and probably is some kind of street thug. For all you know, he might have killed somebody."

"John Doe is not a thug."

She left out the part about how she thought he was the most thrilling man she had met in a very long time. He had charisma plus he had a mysterious past. He was intriguing to her in a way Chester could never be.

She didn't like knowing he'd been a victim of violent crime, but she did like the fact that his misfortune had turned into something good: their encounter together. The subtle difference wasn't lost on Chester.

Daisy kept telling herself that Chester was a good friend even though lately he kept harassing her about her decision to help John Doe. She was already helping him, so what was all the continued fuss about?

"Have you been spending a lot of time with him, Daisy?" Chester asked. The question came off hoarse, intense.

She placed her hands on her hips. "Every chance I get. I figure talking might help him remember parts of his past."

"Does it?"

"Yes. Mostly I've noticed he hasn't forgotten world events, for example. When we watch the news, he understands what's happening and why."

"I think he's faking amnesia."

"Not according to Dr. Randal. Personal family history is missing, but part of it is coming back. He's remembering a woman who's probably his mother. Her name is DeAnn. He also remembers someone named Rosa."

Chester paced a few turns. He came back to stand in front of Daisy. "That's not good enough."

"Say what?"

"Nothing ever is good enough when it comes to you. I want you for myself, Daisy. You have to know by now we belong together."

Daisy's eyes bugged out. It was her turn not to believe what she was hearing. "You can't be serious."

"I'm very serious. I didn't push my luck with you because there was never any competition. John Doe changed all that."

Daisy stretched a hand to the lowest point she could reach on her left shoulder blade to work the kink of frustration out of it. She had physical kinks, emotional kinks, and to top things off, there was a missing person case to solve. "We've got more to lose here than friendship, Chester."

"It's why I'm being honest with you now. I have everything to lose. A man knows when another man is interested in his woman."

"I'm not your woman."

"You would be if he wasn't here."

Daisy took a turn at pacing. When she came back she said, "That's where you're wrong, Chester. I love you like a friend. That's all."

"I don't believe you."

"I'm sorry. I don't mean to hurt you."

His eyes burned into hers. "You're dumping me for a man you just met? I can't believe this is happening."

"I'm not dumping you. We were never a couple. As far as what you believe, I can't help that, either. I didn't lead you on. We've never kissed or talked about anything intimate. I have nothing to feel guilty or ashamed about in our time together. Our relationship has been strictly platonic."

"What proof do you have that this guy won't hurt you, Daisy?"

"None."

"I would never hurt you."

"You're hurting me now with all this talk about me being your woman. I'm not your woman. The way things are going I doubt we're going to be friends for much longer."

Chester had a one-track mind: He was determined to destroy John Doe's credibility in Daisy's eyes. "You also don't have proof this guy has amnesia. You don't have proof he isn't guilty of some crime," he drilled out.

"You're right. I don't have proof. What I've got is a good heart, a sound mind, and a strong sense of judgment. John Doe is being up-front with me."

"John Doe," he mimicked. "You don't even call him John."

"By calling him John Doe, I constantly remind myself he's a lost man in a strange city and that he needs a helping hand."

"I suppose that means when he's ready to sleep with you, you'll let him climb right into your bed."

Daisy slapped him. "Get. Out."

Chester snarled at her. "Did you slap him when he kissed you?"

"What I do with John Doe is none of your business. We're through, Chester. You're fired. I'll mail you your last check in the morning."

"Damn you."

"Damn yourself. Go!"

Chester got three steps to the door before he whirled around. "Not until I take a piece of you with me."

He grabbed Daisy by the shoulders. He kissed her so hard her lips ground against her teeth. She tasted her own blood.

"Chester, don't!"

"Don't what, Daisy? Don't want you? Don't dream about you?"

He crushed her against his chest. He tried to kiss her again but this time, when his lips landed on hers, she bit him. Chester flung her away from him so hard she crashed against the seed rack.

She started to run.

Chester charged after her. He was on her in an instant. Frightened, Daisy screamed.

John Doe burst through the door. In a few steps he was on Chester. In a blink he was punching Chester's face left and right. Chester started punching back.

Cutie Pie heard the ruckus. She charged through the open garden shop door. Once she determined Daisy was safe, Cutie Pie watched the men duke it out.

Daisy was safe but she was ticked off. Chester and John Doe were tearing up the joint. She couldn't have grown men fighting in her establishment. She had worked too hard for too long to build a successful business only to have a pair of macho fools tear it down in the space of a few minutes.

She got a water bucket.

She filled the bucket with cold water.

She threw the water at them.

The men broke apart gasping from the unexpected coldness of the water. "Both of you, listen up," she said. Her voice was as cold as the water she'd run from the hose outside the garden shop door. "I won't have any fighting. I won't have you tearing up my place. Clean this crap up and meet me in the kitchen. Both of you."

John Doe said, "No, Daisy. He's leaving."

Chester stabbed John Doe in the chest with the point of his index finger. "You're the one who's leaving."

Daisy interrupted the two men. "You both are leaving if you don't clean this mess up and meet me in the kitchen like I told you to do. You've got ten minutes." When the men didn't move, she said, "Nine minutes and thirty seconds."

She walked out.

Men, she thought. Sometimes they were real jerks.

She had no proof John Doe was a crook no matter how ugly a picture Chester tried to paint. The lack of proof was what eased her conscience about her relationship with John Doe. No proof meant she could believe him when he told her he was a victim of circumstance.

No proof meant she could keep on enjoying his quiet strength.

Daisy pressed her hand against her forehead. She had a lot to think about when it came to Chester. She had fired him because they couldn't work together. They couldn't work together because she didn't trust him anymore.

She had hoped Chester would be able to harness his aggression long enough for John Doe to get on his own feet. He obviously couldn't. She wondered what could make him wild enough to treat her so crudely. Was his problem jealousy, envy, or something more sinister?

Either way, his behavior shed new light on John Doe's character. He'd had ample time to seduce or even abuse her but he'd never been anything but kind. Chester, the man she trusted, had not only been unkind, he had drawn first blood.

Even if John Doe remembered his real name in the morning and left by the same afternoon, there would still be Chester's negative behavior to deal with. Daisy just didn't see how they could be friends anymore, not when she didn't trust him.

She'd be a fool to do that.

The highway in front of Daisy's Rose and Garden Shop

was quiet when she headed to the house. The other major businesses nearby had shut down for the night. It was the perfect time, Daisy thought, for some chamomile tea.

It surprised her to see a dented white Ford Econoline van heading up the driveway in her direction. To her utter disbelief one of the men had a gun.

She screamed, more from the shock of the gun than true fright; she just couldn't believe what was happening. Who would want to hurt her? Certainly nobody in Guthrie. Briefly, she thought about Chester and knew she could be wrong.

While her mouth yelled big-time, her feet were stuck to the ground like melted bubble gum on the flat side of slick new pumps. She couldn't breathe. She couldn't think. When she found her voice again, what she said didn't make much sense.

She said, "SOMEBODY--ANYBODY—SOME-BODY—PLEASE!"

Cutie Pie heard her. The shepherd ran to the van and started barking.

John Doe heard her. So did Chester. The men exploded from the shop so hard, the glass storm door came right off the hinges.

John Doe hollered, "Move it! Move it! Move it!"

Daisy headed straight for him. In her haste to reach the safety of his powerful body, she dropped her purse. She stumbled over it, skinned a knee on the sidewalk, righted herself, and rasped, "John Doe! Run!"

John Doe didn't say a word. There was no point in saying a word; he wasn't leaving without her. He ran all right, but toward the van. Its smoked-glass windows were the stuff of nasty nightmares, the kind of fright-filled dreams he'd been having without telling Daisy about them.

His memory was coming back.

What he had been remembering wasn't good.

Two nasty-looking thugs burst from the van as if they were twin rockets breaking sound and speed barriers. They fit Miss Tilly's description of the men who'd been to Sonic on Thursday night.

Kickstarted by fear, Daisy made for the opposite direction in a wild bid to gain more time.

She had always felt safe on her property, even with the mysterious John Doe on-site, but tonight her business at the edge of town was a problem. There were no immediate neighbors to hear her scream for help.

This was more than a John Doe job, especially since it was probably John Doe the men in the van were after. He was the only person around with killer enemies. Daisy needed the police—and Chester.

Where was Chester?

She rolled under a billowing bank of pink Betty Prior roses, all the while fumbling for the top-loading zipper on her tan leather purse. She opened the purse to search its jumbled depths to snag two items: her cellular phone and her truck keys.

She shoved the silver ring of her keychain over her thumb to hang on to it.

Cellular phone in hand, Daisy punched the digits 9-1-1.

She knew there was a different set of numbers to dial, but she couldn't think of what they were, star something— but it didn't matter, 9-1-1 would do. One ring. Two rings. Four rings later, an operator answered the line in time to hear her shout into the mouthpiece, "Murder!"

The single word was so universal, so clear to the mind, Daisy felt sure it would bring help on the double. She barely squeezed out the address before 160 pounds of man hauled her from under the Betty Priors.

She used her fists to flail at the man in vain. She didn't know what the men wanted, but it didn't look good. Where, oh where, she wondered, was Cutie Pie? She had been barking when the van showed up.

Now she wasn't barking at all.

No shots had been fired.

She couldn't have been injured.

"Cutie Pie!" Daisy yelled. "Cutie Pie!"

Less than ten yards from Daisy, the fine hairs on John Doe's neck rose like the hackles on an avenging dog. He could feel Daisy's terror, hear her gasps for breath as she struggled against her attacker.

The wild tension building in his gut brought out the superhuman strength inside his body. John Doe surged forward toward Daisy with all the willpower he had in his possession. Nothing would happen to her that wouldn't be avenged this night, not one thing.

A sense of outrage consumed him. He shut down his intellectual self, keyed into the absolute primitive man, the natural, involuntary impulse to either run or fight. He chose to fight, and the enemy of the moment was time. If he was too slow in helping Daisy, she might be seriously hurt.

He couldn't let that happen.

He had to work against time, that ultimate, metered system of reckoning, the part of living that made it possible to even scores and settle accounts.

John Doe zeroed in on his number one agenda: keeping

Daisy alive with time ticking away against them. He had noticed the gun and also that neither man chose to use it. Strange.

Where was Chester?

Where was Cutie Pie?

Daisy could hardly believe her eyes; she blinked them once, she blinked them twice. The man she was growing to love had come to her and was fighting to the death to keep her from harm.

His angry image was of the devil himself.

Daisy felt an intense, almost overpowering sense of relief.

"Get him, John Doe!" she cheered, "Get him!"

The sound of her voice—scared, angry, hopeful— pushed John Doe into the fray without the tiniest shred of thought to his own safety. He understood then, his relationship with Daisy was rooted in something bigger, something deeper than them both.

In spite of everything, she had total faith in him. Her strong belief in him made John Doe feel invincible. Reason clicked down to nothing for him as a long, hairy arm caught Daisy around the neck, tilting her head up at an awkward angle.

She tried to bite the arm that captured her, but the man put her neck in a choke hold. He used the hold to jerk her hard against his chest. She couldn't pull away. It was a difficult battle, and Daisy was losing ground fast.

A blur of spit and fury, John Doe lunged at her attacker, the fierce strength of his hands yanking away the arm pressed against Daisy's throat.

John Doe's victim was frantic to escape. He yelled to his accomplice, "Shoot this mother! Shoot him!"

Right when the villain aimed the gun, the sound of police sirens coming fast and close changed his mind.

The attackers took off.

Daisy slumped to the ground in relief. Just then, Chester came out from behind the bushes. He had Cutie Pie. As soon as he let her go, the German shepherd dashed to Daisy.

John Doe glared at Chester. He registered the smirk on Chester's face. He glanced from Chester's smirk to his own empty hands. He was glad he didn't have a gun. He'd probably shoot him.

Once the police left after questioning them, Daisy took one look at John Doe's face and said, "You remember."

"Yes."

"Let's get cleaned up. Then we can talk."

"Sounds good."

They left the living room, the site of the police interview, at the same time. She headed toward her bedroom. He headed toward the guest room. Cutie Pie's nails clicked against the wood floor. She had refused to leave Daisy's side for any reason. Every time the dog saw Chester, she bared her teeth. Daisy had sent him home.

Home.

By tomorrow morning, that's where John Doe would be. Home. Daisy stopped at her bedroom door. Without glancing back, she asked, "What's your name?"

"Kenneth. Kenneth Gunn."

Kenneth changed into his original clothing. Never again would he wear anything of Chester's. As he changed, Kenneth recalled what had happened to him prior to getting himself beat up and dumped into Daisy's garden.

The driver of the Econoline van had been the same driver of the Impala. Because he recognized the men in the van, Kenneth had been able to give Spud Gurber a complete description.

Kenneth sat on the edge of the queen-size bed in Daisy's guest room. Memories flickered through his mind like old film. He let the tape roll into a flashback. . . .

It was a late May evening in Wichita, Kansas.

A private investigator, Kenneth, arrived at the scene of a terrible crime. There had been a nervous tension in his body that had little to do with the gawking spectators, the flashing patrol car lights, or the dead woman who lay at the center of all the commotion.

Ned Rosa was the homicide detective in charge of the crime scene. He was also Kenneth's best friend.

Ned finished speaking with the medical examiner who presided over the young woman's body. He walked to the tire-scuffed curb where Kenneth waited for him, the senior detective's tough-guy face expressionless, an unlit cigar bent in the middle by a meaty clenched fist. "I want the guy who did this. I want him bad."

Kenneth registered the deep level of vengeance in the homicide detective's voice. The open display of anger was definitely not Ned's usual run-by-the-book self, which was the reason Kenneth stated in trademark, Sidney Poitier calm, "You really think Dr. Thrill did it?"

Haggard from the drama, unkempt by nature, Ned lit a cigar with all the vigor of a man dangling over the crooked line between right and wrong. "I know he did it." Stubby fingers jabbed the cigar between lips curled in disgust. "I just can't prove it."

Kenneth's eyes narrowed at the implication of the senior homicide detective's statement: Ned, a sworn officer of the local law, had more on his mind than simple justice for the deceased. *"What's the deal?"* Kenneth asked.

"The deal"—Ned lowered his voice so that no member of the hardworking crime scene team could hear his volatile remarks—*"I don't wanna pussyfoot around a bunch of red tape before I get my hands on this guy. That's an undercover policewoman on her way to the morgue, not some Jane Doe. This is personal, Kenneth."*

"I hear you."

Ned sucked off a long drag of glowing tobacco as if his peace of mind depended on it, which it did. *"What I need from you is a tie between Dr. Thrill and Vanessa. I need a tie quick. I've got a hunch Dr. Thrill is the perp. I gotta back that hunch up righteous."*

Dr. Thrill was a high-level crime king who was untouchable. He used young women, sex, and drugs to manipulate business deals.

Kenneth said, *"Dr. Thrill is a suspect because he plays dirty business and doesn't treat his women right—"*

Ned cut him off. *"I'm not talking women, damn it, I'm talking about Vanessa. This was her first undercover assignment."* The tough detective with the smoker's rasp and the profound grief had a catch in his voice. *"Dear God! Vanessa."*

"—but being mean and playing dirty don't prove motive or opportunity in a capital murder case."

Ned nearly incinerated with suppressed violence. He was a man who had sworn to protect the public, yet had *failed to protect a member of his own police family. Not all the rage storming through the senior detective's body was against the villain.*

A portion of the rage was against himself, but Ned aimed most of the negative energy at a better target: Vanessa Conrad's killer. "I used her. Dr. Thrill abused her." He spoke each word distinctly, spit it out like a curse.

"Vanessa was undercover," Kenneth pointed out. "It was her job to let him use her. It's up to your detectives to figure out how she ended up getting killed. I'm a private cop. This isn't my case."

Years of training kept Ned from decking his former protégé. He wanted cooperation without hesitation. Ned wanted Kenneth to do what he wanted out of loyalty, but Kenneth followed no man with blind eyes.

"You bastard," Ned said, as much in admiration as in disgust.

Kenneth's dark eyes flickered at the insult. "What do you want from me?"

"Your freedom."

In unison, the men strolled away from the crime scene team. Their conversation had gone too deep for them to remain where they were.

Beneath a street lamp several yards away, Kenneth spoke. "You called me to the crime scene before the victim's body was bagged. Why? Because you want me to see with the eyes of a cop, then act with the freedom of a man in business for himself. Working inside the law is your red tape. Doing the right thing is mine. Even a private cop has rules, Ned. I won't break them, even for you."

The men grew silent.

Around them, newspaper reporters and television me-

dia scavenged the crime scene for bits of blood and gore to spike their late-night news broadcasts.

Civilians huddled in tight groups to discuss the ugly aspects of the lurid event. Police managed the security and protection of evidence while their leader, Ned Rosa, sought an uneasy alliance with a wary friend.

Doing the right thing meant walking a thin line.

Kenneth drew the line.

Ned walked it when he said, "I want indisputable proof Dr. Thrill is behind Vanessa's murder. I don't care how you get it."

Kenneth detached his feelings from the moment. Ned was a man he trusted. Right now Kenneth's trust was being manipulated to fuel the conflict posed by Vanessa's murder.

Lack of proof was the conflict of the moment. Public versus private investigation the complication, a long-time, very meaningful friendship the ultimate risk. "If proof is out there," Kenneth promised, "I'll get it."

Ned pulled a slow drag from his cigar, then released it in a whoosh. "You're here precisely because you don't make things up. As for me"—Ned studied the wet tip of his bent cigar— "I'm tempted."

Respect for his old mentor prompted Kenneth to make his position in the murder investigation totally clear. "I was a cop long enough to know how the system works. Too much of the time it's not about justice but burden of proof and savvy defense lawyers. So like I said, if Dr. Thrill is guilty, I'll get the dirt, make sure it sticks once he goes to trial and his lawyers coach him on how to look innocent."

Ned threw his half-finished cigar to the oil-slick ground, stomping it once with a black leather shoe.

"Don't get me wrong," he said, vengeance low-key but steady in his voice, "I want that bastard to stand trial."

Kenneth was skeptical. His left brow lifted a fraction. Red lights flashed off the parked police cruisers and into his mind. Trouble brewed, he sensed. Big trouble. "Tell me what you've got."

Ned reached behind his back, stuck a hand in his pants pocket, drew out a beat-up wallet, extracted a wrinkled dollar bill, then spoke with false camaraderie. "Let's do this official."

Tension between the men escalated.

Ned sidestepped his legal limitations by handing Kenneth the money, all his hopes for justice meted out through one simple business transaction. He said, "You've just been hired by a friend of Vanessa Conrad."

Kenneth took the wrinkled dollar bill, stuck the money in his pocket, and decided Ned Rosa was as sly as a jackal on the prowl. A friend, as in anybody, perfect cover for a highly respected, highly decorated officer of the local law, a thread which had originally brought the men together in a teacher-student mode that had evolved over the years into a solid friendship, a friendship that murder put to the ultimate test.

If Kenneth succeeded in finding solid proof about the suspected identity of the murderer, the relationship between the old friends would survive.

If he found no evidence to connect the suspect when Ned was convinced he should and would find evidence, their friendship would probably come to a bitter, ugly end.

Kenneth braced himself with a cleansing breath. The terms of their contract had been set: no lies, only the truth. He said, "I'll do it."

Ned walked away without looking back.

Deep thought furrowed the dark plane of Kenneth's forehead as he assessed Vanessa Conrad's murder beyond the physical facts being listed and managed by the crime scene team. Two key details jockeyed for position at the top of his methodical mind:

1) The victim was reported missing several days prior to the discovery of her body. Had the victim disappeared by will or by abduction?

2) The victim died from manual strangulation, her nude body rolled in a carpet and dumped near the trash bin on the side of a trendy boutique. Someone called police with the location of the crime scene. Was the caller a witness? Or a killer?

Kenneth faded into the crowd as the final forensic details were gathered, logged, and protected by police professionals for immediate study. He wasn't worried about those types of crime scene details because those facts were already within Ned Rosa's legal scope and jurisdiction.

Kenneth wanted to study the crowd without any prejudice other than the anger he felt over a young woman's brutal death. What he gleaned from the crowd of police and spectators alike were sharp nerves covered with raw tension.

The tension filled Kenneth with foreboding; the dark dread throwing chills around him felt like tentacles of cold sweat from a nightmare, a bad dream that had a nasty beginning and perhaps a bitter end.

He studied the victim. It struck him Vanessa hadn't been propped up or positioned with care. She had been thrown to the ground beside the large square Dumpster as if she no longer had value to the person who threw her there.

Even if her death had been accidental, disposal of the body had been nothing short of malicious. The careless way Vanessa had been dumped also presented Kenneth with another clue: The body inside the carpet was probably too heavy to toss so freely without help. The ex-cop lifted his eyes to study the growing crowd, a terrible idea gaining weight in his mind: The killer had an accomplice.

That night, Kenneth received a call from Ned. "I've gotta lead," said the senior homicide detective.

"Tell me."

"We checked out Vanessa's apartment. In her notes, we found a clue. Her notes indicated Dr. Thrill had a friend who supplied him with happy pills for his clients."

"Where's the friend?"

"Guthrie, Oklahoma."

"I'll start there."

"Kenneth?"

"Yeah."

"I'll call you in a week or so. If you've got anything before then, call me."

Kenneth stuffed a few toiletry items into a dark Nike sports bag. It wasn't unusual for him to be gone for days at a time, which was the reason he kept no plants or pets. He climbed into his car, a late-model black Impala.

One day later, he was a guest at Daisy's Rose and Garden Shop. . . .

His mind in the present once again, Kenneth realized how lucky he'd been to land in Daisy's compost pile. He was lucky because even though his memory loss had slowed him down, the side issues of Vanessa Conrad's murder had moved parallel to his recovery.

The men who'd tackled and beaten him were Dr. Thrill's men.

Dr. Thrill had murdered Vanessa or arranged to have her murdered.

The men had returned to finish the job they'd started on Kenneth, but hadn't succeeded. They should have succeeded. They had guns and opportunity. The fact he and Daisy were still alive was important.

Kenneth intended to find out why, after two opportunities to be killed, he was still alive.

Fifteen

Daisy joined Kenneth in the living room.

She wore a cream-colored lounge suit made of soft cotton. Her feet were bare. Her hair hung loose to the top of her shoulders. Her face was free of makeup. She felt that like her, the rest of the world held its breath in suspense to learn the secrets of Kenneth's identity.

He sat in a soft chair across from her. The large rectangular coffee table stood between them. There was no chamomile tea or coffee on the glass tabletop, only magazines about gardening, a candle that wasn't lit, and the remote control of the television set.

The lamps in the living room were set on high. There was no music in the background. Despite the fact neither of them wore shoes and both were informally dressed, this meeting was strictly business.

There was the truth to discuss, perhaps even their future.

Cutie Pie lay on her personal cushion in a corner of the living room. She rested on her side in total peace, eyes closed, tail down, muscles relaxed. The German shepherd didn't snarl at Kenneth the way she had snarled at Chester before Daisy kicked him off her property for good after the police had taken his statement.

Daisy accepted Cutie Pie's behavior around Kenneth as a positive sign. If Cutie Pie didn't trust Kenneth, there was no way she would let her guard down, especially after the traumatic event they had all experienced together.

Tonight was about the truth.

Daisy's voice was soft. "Tell me who you are."

"My name is Kenneth Steven Gunn. I'm in my thirties. Single. No children. No special woman in my life. I live alone in a condo in Wichita, Kansas. I'm a private investigator in business for myself."

So far so good, she reasoned. His instincts about the kind of man he figured himself to be had proven correct. From the beginning he believed he was the type of man who would stay loyal to the woman he loved, the kind of man who would proudly wear his wedding ring if he had one.

Daisy was glad he hadn't been unfaithful to another woman when he'd kissed her. She was equally glad there was no reason to feel guilty she had enjoyed being in his arms. Now that the time had come for Kenneth to leave her, she didn't want him to go.

After a few beats of searching silence, she asked, "What kinds of cases are your specialty?"

"I work a variety of cases."

A variety of cases could range from missing persons, to financial crime, to murder. His answer was too vague. Before they left the living room that night Daisy wanted a crisp understanding of the man she had begun to care about.

"You've got to go deeper than that, Kenneth. Are you talking about a variety of cases like the Kinsey Millhone character in the Sue Grafton mystery series?"

"No. More like Spenser in the Robert Parker mystery series."

She had read the *Spenser* book series and watched the *Spenser: For Hire* television shows. She knew all about the tough guy detective with his even tougher sidekick, Hawk. "I don't picture you as a fighter like Spenser."

Kenneth leaned forward, his elbows on his knees, his expression solemn. "Remember I told you not to fit me into a mold?"

"Yes."

"That's why. Neither one of us knew exactly who I was. There were clues that I was into some sort of law enforcement because of the way I tackled the problem of my missing identity. Our hunch was right. It's the details that we didn't have, like where I learned my knowledge. My style of crime fighting isn't pretty or romantic, Daisy."

"I suppose you're right. Have you been in tougher situations than the one we faced when those guys showed up in the van?"

"I have."

"Wow." She rubbed her arms as if cold. "I don't need any more excitement."

His smile was wry. "Chester was right about one thing."

"What?"

"Even though my brief bout of amnesia was tragic, I'm not a basket case in need of sympathy. He was right to warn you not to think of me as helpless. As you saw tonight, I'm not helpless. I'm a fighter."

Daisy recalled that Robert Parker's character had been a retired boxer. "Do you get into a lot of fistfights the way the Spenser character does?" she asked.

"I've never fought professionally, if that's what you want to know. I fight when I have to fight using whatever weapon suits the job best and only when that kind of force is necessary. Take tonight for example. A simple stop command wouldn't have helped. Those men in the van used excessive force. I used excessive force."

Daisy shivered, not from cold but from what might have happened if the police hadn't shown up when they did. "Those men could have killed us both. Why didn't they?"

"Probably for the same reason I wasn't killed the night the same two men dumped me in your garden. Somebody somewhere wants to keep me alive."

"I'll go along with that." She stopped rubbing her arms. "So what do you think about Chester hiding in the bushes during all the action?"

Kenneth's eyes bored into Daisy's, as if he measured the strength of her loyalty to Chester Whitcomb. He finally said, "Chester wasn't hiding."

Her tone was indignant. "Of course he was hiding."

"No, he wasn't hiding in the bushes, Daisy. It only appeared that way. Do you remember that Cutie Pie was missing for a while?"

"Yes."

"That bothered me." Kenneth measured his next words carefully. "After Spud left with the rest of the police, I took a flashlight and searched the area where Chester had been in the bushes. I found evidence of a scuffle."

"A what?"

"A scuffle. A physical power struggle. The dirt is soft in that area. I noticed it was trampled on. Some prints were human. Some prints were dog prints. Some of the groundcover you've got over there was trampled down also. The little white flowers were crushed."

"Candytuft," she said. "I have a lot of little green plants with tiny white flowers over there. What you think of as groundcover is really candytuft. Are you saying"—her tone was just short of a whisper—"are you saying Chester held Cutie Pie down while those men were fighting with us?"

"He did more than hold her down. I think he muzzled her in some way. I don't remember Cutie Pie barking after she charged into the shop behind me, Daisy. Do you? Once we were outside, Chester and Cutie Pie disappeared."

She thought for a long time. When she responded, her voice was heavy with shock and regret. "I can't believe this, but it makes sense."

Only someone Cutie Pie felt comfortable with would have been able to get close to her, especially during a crisis. Cutie Pie had trusted Chester because Daisy had trusted Chester.

"She didn't run to you until *after* the men in the van took off," Kenneth continued. "She didn't run after them at first because Chester was holding her back by the collar. When he finally let her go, Cutie Pie chased the van off the property before coming back to check on you. I feel honored that she knew you were safe with me."

Daisy rubbed the bridge of her nose with a thumb and forefinger. "She's been snarling at Chester ever since."

"Right."

Her voice dropped an octave. "I'm gonna kill that bastard."

"I wanted to do that myself when I saw the expression

on his face after the police were on the way and the van had taken off."

"And I thought he had just chickened out." Daisy was clearly disgusted. "Wait a minute. You're saying . . . I mean . . . you think Chester knows those men?"

"He had to know them, Daisy. Those men had a gun, but they didn't use it. Chester must have thought my amnesia was permanent or he was just desperate to stop you from caring for me. I'm sure you've noticed how easy we get along together. We think a lot alike. This has to drive Chester crazy. Don't forget that he's in love with you."

"You think maybe they didn't use the gun because Chester didn't want me to be hurt, he just wanted me to be scared?"

"I'd agree with you except for my having seen those men before. Keep in mind that they are the guys who dumped me here."

"Are you telling me that the same guys who were seen driving a black Impala around Guthrie are the same guys who beat you up?"

He nodded his head, his expression intense. "Let me explain. I'd stopped at the business next door to the fast-food drive-in to ask some questions. I'd been following up on a lead about a suspected accomplice to a man called Dr. Thrill."

Daisy swung her feet to the floor. She leaned forward with her elbows on her thighs, her hands clasped tightly together. "I can't believe this. Dr. Who?"

"Thrill."

Her laugh was short and bitter. "This is wild, Kenneth. Nothing like this happens in Guthrie. You're talking about a Dr. Thrill like a . . . like a James Bond bad guy. A Gold-finger type of bad guy."

Kenneth didn't laugh. "More like a Dr. No type of bad guy. Dr. No kept avoiding capture. Like the character Dr. No, we never catch Dr. Thrill, either. We only catch his accomplices."

Daisy jumped to her feet. She paced three steps left and right before standing still again. "You think Chester is this Dr. Thrill?"

"No. I think he works for Dr. Thrill in some way."

"You can't be serious!"

Kenneth stayed seated, but his body was tense. "I'm serious. It's why I came all the way from Wichita. Those goons were already in Guthrie when I got here. To make a long story short, after I ate lunch at Sonic, I walked back to pick up my car. I did some more checking on leads. I was driving down Pine, out past the cemetery, when they carjacked me at gunpoint."

"Hold up," she ordered. "What in the world were you doing at the cemetery?"

"To be honest, I was just driving around. I wanted to get a feel for the town itself. I was trying to figure out why Dr. Thrill would choose an accomplice who lived in such an unlikely place. I was looking at that vacant field on the west side of the cemetery when I noticed the white van."

"How could you let a big old van like that get close to you without noticing it?"

He was clearly embarrassed. He cleared his throat. "Let's just say I made a stupid mistake. I was actually thinking about how I'd like to come back to Guthrie for a visit and really be a tourist. I like the downtown area but I was looking at that open field and wondering how much it would cost to buy something like that. I was daydreaming about a little house and my own pond where I could fish whenever I wanted to and that's how I got caught."

"And then what?"

"I was taken off for some old-fashioned questioning about why I was in town. I drove with a gun to my head while the van followed."

"That's when you got your beating."

He nodded. "We drove a long time on some back country roads. I don't even think we were in Guthrie anymore when we stopped. I was taken to an abandoned building and knocked around for a while. I must have passed out. When I woke up, it was to the taste of compost. You know the rest."

"I still don't understand about your car. Miss Tilly says you were at Sonic eating alone. Without your car. You couldn't have been carjacked before that."

"My car was at the business next door to Sonic."

Daisy saw Sonic all the time, but for a few seconds, she couldn't remember the names of the businesses just before or after it. "You mean the white building that sells mobile phones and pagers?"

He nodded. "Like I said, I'd been following up on a lead there. Instead of driving a few yards to Sonic for lunch, I left my car where it was and walked over. When the two men who beat me up were later seen in the car, they were just joyriding."

"You make it sound so simple."

Kenneth pulled Daisy to the couch so that he could hold her hands. "It is. I've learned that most of the clues

I search for are right at my fingertips. I've just got to keep an open mind in order to see them."

He told her about Ned Rosa and the dead policewoman. "The clue about Dr. Thrill's connection to Guthrie was right there in Vanessa's apartment. Once Ned found the clue and called me, I drove straight here."

"Why didn't you fly?"

"I wanted time to think. Also, I needed my own transportation. I like to keep my work as simple as possible. Guthrie is small. I wanted to blend in with the tourists as much as I could. In a town this size, a guy looking for a rental car would stand out and be remembered."

"How did you find Chester?"

Before he'd been carted off and beaten, Kenneth had been able to glean a few details about the murder Ned Rosa had hired him to investigate. "Chester works with a snitch named Harold. Harold's loyalty isn't to Chester. It's to the man with the most cash in his hand. Vanessa had connected with Harold. Harold is a snitch for Chester. Chester is a pill pusher for Dr. Thrill."

Daisy felt like her head was exploding. "My god! Chester is a trained pharmacist! He'd know all about prescription drugs."

"Right. Prescription drugs sound pretty tame until you really think about it. People forget that common medicines like Tylenol become a controlled substance when mixed with codeine. Just about any medicine can become habit-forming if it's used the wrong way. Dr. Thrill dispenses prescription drugs like candy to his clients."

Daisy felt piece after piece of the mystery coming together. "Spud is always teasing Chester about not using his degree. He's really been using it all along."

"He's using it, all right. If I hadn't been carjacked and beaten half to death, I'd probably know what Chester's been doing with the side money he's earning as Dr. Thrill's accomplice. Dr. Thrill is the guy that intrigues me. I don't know what he looks like or where he lives or why he does what he does."

Kenneth leaned back on the sofa, Daisy's head on his shoulder. In the background, Cutie Pie snored. "Ned Rosa mentioned Dr. Thrill to me a few times in the past. It's a long-standing issue he's been trying to close for years."

"Where does Dr. Thrill get his name?"

"He gets his name because he uses women for thrills and then he kills them. It's why Vanessa was undercover. She was killed before she could tell Ned everything she knew."

Daisy thought Vanessa had been pretty brave to take on such a hard-to-catch career criminal. "She must have had something substantial on Dr. Thrill in order for him to feel threatened enough to kill her."

Kenneth's sigh was deep and long. "Ned is frustrated because he lost a good policewoman. To make things even worse, he's hardly any closer to catching Dr. Thrill now than he was before Vanessa died."

"That's where you're wrong, Kenneth. Ned put you on the trail Vanessa left behind. Her death wasn't in vain."

"I hadn't thought about it that way, but you're right."

Daisy clenched her fists. "I trusted Chester!"

"He wanted you to trust him. Don't feel bad. A lot of the criminals I've met were really nice guys when they weren't dealing in crime. Ted Bundy was a serial killer, but most people he met thought he was a great guy until he was caught and convicted." Kenneth squeezed her hand. "You saw the side of Chester that he wanted you to see, Daisy."

"He was my friend!"

"True. That's why it hurts. Just don't feel guilty. You gave a hardworking man a steady job. Nothing more. Nothing less."

All of that made perfect sense, but she couldn't bottle her feelings up that easily. She and Chester had good memories together. Now the bad memories would forever outweigh the good. "Now what?"

"I need to touch base with Ned. He'll wire me enough funds to get me through the next couple of days and back home again." Kenneth's grin was crooked. "I don't think I'll wear another running suit for a while. I'm gonna stop at Wal-Mart to get some jeans. I can't believe this town only has a Wal-Mart as a major store."

She looked away. *Home.* He had said it so casually. He was leaving. Leaving. She didn't want him to go. "What about Chester?" she asked quietly.

"I'll figure something out with the local authorities. I don't have a license to work in this area. Asking questions around town is one thing. Taking the law into my own hands is something else. I work with the police whenever I need to."

Daisy looked over at Cutie Pie. There had been one other person the German shepherd had been relaxed around that night. "Talk to Spud."

"I will. When he was taking my statement, he told me he was on his way out here anyway when your 9-1-1 call came through police dispatch. That's why he got here so fast. My prints came up with a positive hit. He already knew my name and where I lived. He just hadn't known what I was doing in Guthrie."

"And Kenneth?" Daisy touched her fingers to his face. It was a strong, honest, compelling face to behold. There was so much they didn't know about each other in terms of what each liked to eat, what kinds of music each enjoyed. Yet it was just as he said earlier: They fit well together. They felt right.

"Yeah, Daisy?" His voice was deep, as if he, too, was suddenly conscious that their adventure was nearing its end.

"Be careful."

He pressed her fingers to his cheek. "Don't worry. I can take care of myself. I want you to close the shop for a few days. Keep Cutie Pie with you at all times when I'm not here. I'm going to call Ned tonight. In the morning, I'll visit Spud. He and his cop friends will keep regular cruises down Division. Keep your cell phone handy."

"You aren't afraid Chester will skip town?"

"No."

"Why?"

"He has roots in Guthrie. You're part of the reason he stays. I want you to stay put inside the house. It won't take me long to do what I've got to do at the police station in the morning. Keep Cutie Pie in the house, too. She won't let Chester near you ever again."

"You just do whatever you have to do," she advised. "You've got a case to solve. I can handle Chester."

She rubbed her hands together as if she couldn't wait to get her hands around his neck.

Kenneth wanted to do more than wring Chester's neck. He wanted to kill him.

Sixteen

It was the next afternoon. Kenneth had been gone a couple of hours. Off duty, Spud had picked him up so that Daisy wouldn't be without her car in case she needed to make a quick getaway, even though Spud had assured her that Guthrie police would continue to keep an eye on her place. Kenneth hadn't wanted to take chances. He insisted she keep her car.

After Kenneth briefed the GPD about his investigation, he and Spud were to head to the Western Union office for the money Ned Rosa had wired. The next stop planned was a trip to Wal-Mart for an overnight bag, toiletry items, underclothes, two casual shirts, and two pairs of jeans. Kenneth expected to be on his way home in two days.

Two days.

At the house, the idea she might not see Kenneth again drove Daisy from the safety of her living room to the sanctuary of her private garden, the one she reserved for her personal use and for the pleasure of close family and friends.

This private space was her secret garden, located through the French doors off the master bedroom.

In her secret garden, among the roses and their companion plants, Daisy found peace of mind. She needed to connect with her own inner stillness, her own self-protection system. She didn't need a man to make her strong. To feel strong, she relied on her own self-confidence, her own will, her own reason. Being with Kenneth Gunn made her feel energized, more vibrant than her usual self. She would feel restless once he was gone.

In Wichita, Kansas, he had a career, family, friends. He had a life.

In the beginning he would think of her, but in the end, the familiarity of his normal routines would claim his full attention once again.

Daisy was no bleeding heart; she was a realist with a conscience. Realists kept both eyes open, not one eye closed.

Routine. Rituals. Comfort.

Dressed in her usual jeans and cotton top, Daisy kicked off her green rubber garden clogs. Her feet bare, she concentrated on the feel of crabgrass. She hated crabgrass. In warm weather months, pulling crabgrass from the ground was a great way to vent frustration. On this day, it was a safe enemy to tackle on her own.

On her hands and knees, Daisy pulled stray grass without benefit of her gardening gloves. The grass felt cool and tough against her skin. As she worked away at the weeds she found, she gained a sense of comfort.

Beetles and crickets and spiders scurried among the mulch she disturbed, reminding her that some things never changed. No matter how much compost and rotted cow manure and cypress mulch she laid out in the garden, there were still imperfections that marred the beauty of the roses she loved.

Weeds still found a way to thrive. Insects devised new ways to adapt to the changes she made in the soil and the plants that grew in the soil. Weeds and insects were like problems—as soon as one disappeared, another one took its place.

After the drama died down, after Chester was caught for his crimes, after Kenneth had returned to Wichita, Kansas, and after all the gossip died down, she would still have her garden. She would still have crabgrass.

There would be beetles and crickets and spiders and gossip to remind her that Guthrie was still Guthrie. It was still home. No matter what happened, Guthrie was where she belonged. She loved who she was and the life she had built for herself.

She had a business she adored, a business that was a haven not only for herself, but for the other plant lovers in town who considered Daisy's Rose and Garden Shop a home away from home.

She had a life, too.

On a small patio table behind her, a compact disc player finished its collection of metaphysical songs by David Lanz. When the music stopped playing, Daisy got off her hands and knees.

Refreshed, she felt ready to return to the house again. She had a taste for chocolate and planned to make her favorite cake: chocolate delight. She turned around and froze.

Seated in a chair beside the patio table was Chester Whitcomb. He had a toothpick in his mouth. She had no idea how long he'd been there. It could have been twenty minutes. It could have been five.

Daisy didn't bother to ask how he had come in. She had treated him as a close friend. Close friends sometimes knew about spare keys, unlocked windows, garage codes, and security quirks.

As a close friend, Chester knew all about her secret garden. He knew she listened to David Lanz as a form of relaxation while she tended her personal getaway space. He knew that her getaway space was actually a quarter of an acre in size.

There were high wood walls to separate her private garden from her public garden. Her secret place was decorated with clematis-covered pergolas, a rambling grapevine, five-foot-tall hollyhocks, and giant delphinium.

There were weather-worn wooden benches backed by pink ballerina roses, a small fish pond, a shed for her tools. A man could hide in her garden. Obviously, that is what Chester had done.

Twenty feet away, beneath a rose of Sharon heavy with flower pods, Cutie Pie slept in the shade, relaxed by the familiar ritual of Daisy tending her garden to the sound of instrumental music. The dog was not on guard.

Daisy knew the only way Chester would have a chance to hurt her was if he had a gun. If she called out, Cutie Pie would come. It would take less than fifteen seconds for the dog to reach her mistress. Signaling Cutie Pie would signal the beginning of violence. Daisy hated violence. Chester knew this, too.

Gun or no gun, friend or foe, one way or another, she vowed this would be her last confrontation with Chester. Never again would he find refuge in her garden or in her life. Damn him. Damn him for being the snake in her paradise.

She said as calmly as she could, "Don't do this."

He glanced at Cutie Pic.

Returning his gaze to Daisy, Chester placed one long finger to his lips in a warning for her to stay quiet. Would she yell? Or would she walk quietly with him through the French doors and into a reality of his making?

Anticipation was as clear on his face as the sun that shined down on them both. For Chester Whitcomb, this was opportunity.

The next move was up to Daisy. In the quiet, she heard birds moving in the shrubs, leaves rustling on the trees, traffic pushing up Highway 77, the road in front of her house.

Fight or flight? It was Russian roulette.

Trust. Click.

Trust. Click.

Trust. Click.

Betrayal.

Chester sidled over to her, hooked an index finger beneath her chin, lifted her face to his and said, "I remembered how you like to come here to be alone when you want to relax."

When Daisy snatched her chin from his too-familiar touch, Chester added, "I came to chat."

She wanted to knock him off his feet. Her voice low and mean, she said, "You must be crazy."

His gaze was totally unreadable. Chester had stuck around Daisy because he liked her spunk. She wasn't needy. She wasn't asking for children or a husband or a house or a car or for protection. She was self-contained and self-sufficient.

Oh, how she thrilled him with her spirited ways, her

deep passion for all things she cared about. He found that no other woman equaled her. No other woman treated him the same way or better.

He fingered a strand of her unbound hair. "Let's start over."

Discord and disquiet electrified Daisy's mind. She wanted to run, but she couldn't, not from her carefully constructed life, her family, her future. She wanted to build on her fresh start with Kenneth.

Thinking of Kenneth gave Daisy strength.

She said, "I know about you and Dr. Thrill. You're involved with the murder of a Kansas policewoman."

Chester had come to her with everything to lose, everything to gain. In contrast, Kenneth had come to her with nothing and had won everything. Having everything meant having her trust.

Chester hated losing Daisy's faith in him. It was something he had taken for granted. "I'll make you want me again."

This thought was his obsession.

She trembled. Chester cared nothing for what she wanted. If he did, he would have walked away from her and stayed gone. Instead, he had waited until she let her guard down, until he knew she was alone, wrapped in her thoughts and her dreams.

He had waited for Cutie Pie to settle into her favorite spot beneath the rose of Sharon. Their combined distraction had worked to his benefit, and now Daisy was in trouble. Big trouble. She could feel it.

The idea he wanted to harm her was unnerving. That he was possibly a murderer chilled her to the bone. "You act like we were lovers. It's too late for us. I don't trust you anymore. You used me, Chester."

Even after all that had gone wrong between them, he was surprised she discounted their past so easily. They had spent many nights by the fire, just talking. His tone was tight, rigid. "We belong together, Daisy."

Anger quickened her voice. "Get away from me."

Chester made a grab for her left arm. His voice menaced her. "You're saying this because of that ex-cop." The last word was spit from his tongue like an epithet, as if bitter to the taste and to the mind.

She tried to snatch her arm away, but he held the flesh tight.

Forcing her body to relax, she asked, "Is that why you sent those goons? You're pissed off you didn't get your way and decided to scare me instead?"

He released her arm, flexed his fingers. His eyes were too bold, too rough, too vicious. "I'm here to talk about us."

Chester's obsession, that beast of desire that troubled his mind, grew more brazen with each stroke of his slippery tongue. At last, Daisy was within his control. At last, he spoke his true mind. He felt triumphant.

Daisy watched the transformation in him with horror. "You're scaring me."

For the first time since accosting her, Chester relaxed. She seldom admitted feeling vulnerable. "Good."

Daisy couldn't believe her predicament. There she was, standing in her own backyard, scared spitless.

She glared at Chester for crashing, unwanted, into her life yet again, for wrecking her peace, for shattering her illusion of safety.

Comfort was as far away from her now as the sun.

She said, "What do you mean, *good?*"

"If you're scared," he explained, "you'll pay attention."

Anger broke Daisy's fear into small bits of tension. "What I'll do, Chester, is press charges."

His lust for her glared brightly. Beauty, brains, passion, business savvy—she was the kind of powerhouse woman a man could build on. "I've always liked your guts, Daisy, but as you can see, I've got the upper hand."

Her eyes cut him to pieces. "We never were really friends. If I couldn't get it through my head before, I sure can get it through my head now."

His silence fed the malice which fed the greed which made his love an obsession. True fear, he knew, had yet to reach her, but it would, he vowed. It would. "We're just getting started."

"There have to be other women who interest you."

Chester's skin was taut over the strong bones of his face. "I don't want another woman."

"Is that what happened to Vanessa Conrad? You didn't want to let her go so you killed her?"

Malice knew its time, and the time had come.

Chester opened one side of his lightweight, expensive jacket to reveal a gun in his waistband, a short-barreled gun. His right eye ticked once, then again. Moving slowly, almost distractedly, he removed the revolver and caressed her left cheek with the tip of it.

Daisy's cheek quivered. Her muscles felt like jelly. She wanted one last chance to tell her mother good-bye. She hadn't done more than talk to her mother on the phone in the last few days.

She never had made the time to take Kenneth to see

the special rose in her mother's garden. The most special rose was and always would be Daisy's own mother. It was the only part of her mother's garden that could never be replaced.

Daisy glared at Chester as if she had X-ray vision. "Kenneth is gonna kill you," she said, "if I don't kill you first."

Chester smiled, cold and hateful. "Look at you. You're scared, but you're playing it off like you're running the show. I've always admired your spunk, Daisy, but let's face it, we've got a problem."

"Wrong. I don't have a problem. You do."

Daisy whistled.

Cutie Pie went from a dead sleep to a dead run. She didn't bother to bark or growl. She just kept coming.

For three precious seconds, Chester froze. In those three seconds, Daisy had the advantage.

She knocked the gun from his hand. Before Chester could get to the French doors, the dog was on him.

Chester—tough, crime-dealing Chester—screamed.

Daisy stared at him as if she had never seen him before. She thought she had known him, but she hadn't. It was Chester who had been the truly mysterious one in her life. In contrast, Kenneth had been honest, forthright, focused, and kind.

She wanted to help him solve the case which had brought him into her life. For that, she needed Chester in one piece. "Cutie Pie. Stop!"

Cutie Pie pretended she couldn't hear Daisy. She kept right on chewing Chester up. Chester kept on screaming. As yet, no blood had been drawn. Cutie Pie was still in warning mode.

Daisy chucked the gun into the bushes with the birds. Kenneth had said he would be gone for only a few hours. He'd been gone for three. He'd be back soon.

Daisy pulled up a chair. She sat down. Realizing that Cutie Pie wasn't trying to kill him, Chester stopped screaming. As long as Daisy wasn't upset, Cutie Pie wouldn't kill him. The way to keep Daisy from being upset was to keep his cool.

Chester wondered if luck was on his side. He wondered if he would get away one last time without being caught. He wondered if Kenneth Gunn was even now using the spare key to walk through Daisy's front door.

Then Chester remembered. Kenneth couldn't have her spare key. The spare key was in his pocket. He had used the key to enter her house in the first place. He had to get rid of Cutie Pie. If only he could move.

Tick . . . tock. . . . tick . . . tock . . . tick.

Chester couldn't believe she was just sitting there. He laughed in spite of his bad situation. "Daisy, I'm gonna hate wringing your beautiful little neck."

"Did you hate ringing Vanessa Conrad's neck?"

"No. She had it coming."

Daisy was stunned. "You admit you killed her?"

"Why not?" he countered. "You won't be telling anybody."

Kenneth heard every word. He was the real reason Cutie Pie hadn't gobbled Chester up. He had arrived on the scene at the point just before Daisy had thrown the gun in the bushes. Cutie Pie hadn't listened to Daisy because she was taking her cues from Kenneth.

The shepherd's shift in behavior wasn't disloyal to her

mistress. In a dog's world, power is established by hierarchy.

Cutie Pie recognized that in the order of things, Kenneth Gunn was the master in charge. The dog continued to protect her mistress, but as any dog understood, there could be only one leader in a pack.

Kenneth stepped out onto the patio. "Daisy won't have to tell. You just did."

Cutie Pie released her grip.

Chester lunged for Kenneth.

Daisy jumped out of the way, ran to the telephone, and called 9-1-1. She explained the problem and asked for Detective Ned Rosa of the Wichita Police Department to be notified of the crime in progress.

Minutes later, the Guthrie police stormed the house, Spud Gurber leading the way. In one glance, Spud understood the drama, the life struggle going on between the two fighting men.

Spud had never walked the line between good cop and bad cop. He was a good cop all the way. "Kenneth!" he shouted. "Enough!"

But it was Daisy who stopped the fight.

She placed a firm hand on Kenneth's arm. Just as he positioned Chester for a terrible blow to the face, her touch brought him back to reality.

With fresh eyes, Kenneth saw what at first he could not see—that he was carefully, methodically beating Chester Whitcomb to death.

Seventeen

Ned Rosa sat with Kenneth in a pair of white motel chairs beneath a six-year-old crabapple tree in Daisy's front yard. As soon as Kenneth had called him the night before, he'd made arrangements to fly from Wichita to Oklahoma City.

At the Will Rogers Airport, Ned had rented an economy car, which he drove to Guthrie and straight to Daisy's house. He'd arrived shortly after Kenneth's fight with Chester.

Ned opened his briefcase, then shuffled through it to find a pen. "I'm gonna cut you a check for expenses."

Kenneth remained silent. There was more going on here than a check for expenses. Ned rarely beat around the bush, which is what Kenneth thought he was doing now. There was no reason to cut a check in Guthrie, Oklahoma for a job that had started in Wichita, Kansas.

Ned pulled a bankbook from the inner breast pocket of his suit jacket. "Your part in this thing is over. Even though you involved civilians in a capital murder investigation, it all worked out for the best."

Ned paused, then spoke his next words carefully. "I want you to know that if you hadn't turned up by now, I would've come out here lookin' for you. Even though you forgot where you started out from, I didn't. We spoke on the phone before you left Wichita for Guthrie to follow up on Vanessa's lead."

"I know."

Ned gazed at the stars. In the absence of skyscrapers, his view of the earth's ceiling was unlimited. Born and raised in a big city, he hadn't known stars could be so bright. "I still can't believe you lost your mind in this one-horse town."

"Amnesia, Ned. I had amnesia."

"I still can't believe it. Just means you're human after all, I guess. You're damn lucky Whitcomb's henchmen only beat the crap out of you when you got too close to him. I bet Whitcomb wished his men had gone on and killed you before they dumped you in that pile of . . . what was it Daisy found you lying in?"

"Compost."

"Yeah. Compost. Anyway, Whitcomb must have freaked when you turned up on Daisy's property. Of all the possible dumping spots in this little town, they had to pick the one spot where he had a close relationship with a beautiful woman. That's a pretty freaky coincidence."

"It's the main reason why Whitcomb didn't want to help me," Kenneth said. "He didn't know how much I knew about him, which was really very little. I knew Dr. Thrill's accomplice was in Guthrie, but the only connection to the accomplice was Harold, the snitch. Whitcomb couldn't afford not to help me. If he had refused, it would have been out of character in the role he played for Daisy. He's such a helpful guy when it comes to her. At least he used to be."

Ned handed Kenneth a check, returned the bankbook

to the inner breast pocket of his gray business suit, and leaned back in his motel chair with a thoughtful look on his face. "The van incident was strange. I don't know what Whitcomb hoped to accomplish."

Kenneth did. "He wanted to run off. If I hadn't been a private cop, I might not have paid as much attention to the details of what happened. A true civilian might have been focused primarily on the attack itself."

"Right. But being a cop, you noticed Whitcomb had disappeared. In your report, you even noted the mental condition of Daisy's dog." Ned flipped through the report on his lap. "Cutie Pie. You said Cutie Pie was outraged with Whitcomb, somebody she should have trusted. A dog doesn't snap at a trusted person without good cause. You made a good observation when you noticed the dog's changed behavior. It was a definite clue that Whitcomb was bad news."

"Thanks. Daisy noticed right away I had the instincts of a cop. Chester knew it for a fact. He was desperate. I think I'm alive today because of my training. Daisy felt from the beginning there was somebody trying to keep me alive."

"Whitcomb."

"Right, but not out of loyalty. Whitcomb knew that if he killed a cop, private or otherwise, he'd always be looking over his shoulder because the heat would be turned up on him. No matter how he looked at it, I was a problem. He was damned if he did anything to me and damned if he didn't. It's no wonder he went after Daisy out of frustration. I just wished I'd had a chance to talk to Harold before Whitcomb made his move on her. Whitcomb knew who I was. I didn't know who he was. Daisy never thought she was in danger. Her ignorance in this case was actually a blessing."

Ned reached for a cigar from the inside of his cluttered briefcase. "The best thing about this mess is that you caught Vanessa Conrad's killer. I thought it would turn out to be Dr. Thrill who did her in, not Dr. Thrill's accomplice, Whitcomb. That Dr. Thrill is a tricky bastard. I just might work something out where you track him down until you bring him down."

"Yeah."

Kenneth knew all about police bureaucracy, short funds, short staff, short tempers. They were the key reasons why Ned had hired him to solve Vanessa Conrad's murder in the first place. Kenneth didn't blame him for wanting to use his services again.

The main reason Kenneth would accept the case to pursue Dr. Thrill was to find out about the woman Chester's henchmen were seen with while they were cruising around in the Impala.

He thought it was probably Dr. Thrill's girlfriend or a replacement for Vanessa. It would suit the emerging profile of Dr. Thrill, who seemed to use other people to do his dirty work. The woman was probably long gone by now.

Kenneth turned his mind to that particular problem. "Spud ran the plates on the van. They were stolen."

It was against the rules of Daisy's Rose and Garden Shop to smoke in nondesignated areas within the public gardens, but Ned lit his stogie anyway. The act of smoking, of inhaling slowly and exhaling even more slowly, kept him calm.

He needed all his wits to catch Dr. Thrill, a man he

viewed as a meticulous bastard who continually got away with murder. He might not have killed Vanessa with his own hands, but Ned felt Dr. Thrill was definitely part of the reason why Vanessa died: She had been investigating him for Ned.

He said in disgust, "Everybody knows Dr. Thrill is as crooked as Whitcomb, but we never have been able to get any dirt on him. He runs that strip joint, the Silver something or other. Rumor has it he's into prostitution. He's got dancers, but the women sometimes see men for sexual favors on the side. That's not prostitution if we can't prove the money the women make goes into Dr. Thrill's pocket. It hasn't been proven. Neither has it been proven that occasionally, when some of his dancers turn up missing and possibly dead, Dr. Thrill had anything to do with it."

Kenneth didn't like where the conversation was headed. He hadn't known Daisy long, but he was a great judge of character. In his line of work, he had to be on target when it came to dealing with the criminal mind. There was nothing criminal about Daisy. It was criminal that Chester had abused her trust, something Kenneth refused to do.

Daisy was intelligent, had a strong head for business, and had been a great friend of Chester Whitcomb's, a friendship that had jeopardized her life, something else Kenneth refused to do. He said, "Daisy stays out of this. I've risked her life enough."

"You didn't risk her life, Kenneth. The way I see it, you probably saved it." Ned took a long drag of his cigar. "Whitcomb killed Vanessa when either he or Dr. Thrill got tired of her. He might have killed Daisy when he decided he didn't want to be around her anymore."

"Daisy isn't Whitcomb's girlfriend, and my landing in

the compost pile was a coincidence," Kenneth said. "I don't think Whitcomb figured out what happened until he rushed to Daisy's aid after she called him the night she found me. When he recognized my face, he became instantly hostile. His total dislike put us at odds from the start. I didn't trust him and he didn't trust me. I thought our rivalry was based on jealousy over Daisy."

"To a large extent, it was," Ned agreed. "You had no memory of why you were in Guthrie, but Whitcomb did. Your lack of memory was your connection to Daisy, the woman Whitcomb had pegged for himself. Sounds like a soap opera."

"I was almost too late to save her."

"But you did. Daisy turned out to be the key to solving the who and the why of Vanessa's murder. I only have one doubt about you taking on the Dr. Thrill case. I haven't forgotten about the mystery woman you think could be his girlfriend. If that's true, my guess is he's using that woman the same way he used Vanessa. Finding her is a mystery for another day, though. You need to get back to Wichita. Those bruises of yours are healing up pretty good, but you still look like crap to me."

Kenneth chuckled. "Daisy says I look great."

"Well." Ned blew more smoke. He took his time forming his response. "That says a lot."

"What do you mean?"

"It says she can't see the bruises anymore because she sees you, the man. That she can make you forget your troubles tells me she's not an ordinary woman. Two weeks ago, you'd have been hightailing after the woman we think might be Vanessa's replacement. Instead, you're willing to go after her later."

"I want to be sure Daisy's safe."

"Huh. Let you tell it." Ned took another drag. He smoked cigars for the same reason Daisy and Kenneth drank coffee—to relax. "The way you've been defending the Rogers chick is proof you're too close to this case, Kenneth my man. You've got to be objective." Ned blew a smoke ring at the sky. "You can't be objective when you're screwing the suspect's friends."

Coldly, precisely, Kenneth shut his face down. He leaned forward in careful, metered increments. He looked Ned straight in the eyes and said, "You're the one who can't be objective. You're so obsessed with catching Dr. Thrill you risked Vanessa's life. You hired me because you felt guilty. When I turned up missing, you thought I was dead, too. Now you want to play it safe by getting me back to Wichita. It's too late to play it safe."

Kenneth's voice dropped, but he didn't move back, didn't back down. "You can't rush me back to Wichita. Dr. Thrill may wish to retaliate for Whitcomb's capture by harming Daisy."

"You'll quit if I pay you off. Which I did."

Kenneth ripped up the personal check. "I can't be bought."

Ned scowled a full ten seconds. He had his stogie working like a chimney for another five seconds. Decision made, he said, "Fine. You're on your own from here out."

Kenneth knew those words were a green light from Ned: Hear no evil, see no evil, get our man—Dr. Thrill. Kenneth said, "Give me a lead."

Ned stared at his stogie, his manner contemplative. "First of all, this Harold character who was a snitch for Vanessa is actually clean. This guy is a small-time thief and a small-time gambler but right now, he's not under investigation for any crime other than having lousy friends. Chester Whitcomb specifically."

Kenneth took his own sweet time mulling over what he'd just heard. Chester was a popular man in Guthrie. It was his popularity that made him legitimate in Daisy's eyes in the first place. Whatever dirty deals occupied Chester's private time, he had been careful to keep them private.

Kenneth leaned his back against the motel chair, legs splayed out in front of him. "It appears that Harold maintains the privacy of his friends at a cost."

"Right now," Ned said, "he's trying to stay out of jail. He started squealing as soon as he found out Daisy had been Whitcomb's target. A man like Harold, who is willing to sell or trade what he knows, is useful."

Kenneth figured Harold's lack of loyalty was a tricky thing. The lack of loyalty made him unreliable. Still, it was a good lead in a case that moved to closure at a snail's pace. "You were going to give me a lead."

Ned was no master of dark and dirty deeds, for all his outward appearances. He had never before tangled with the desire to kill a man for the sake of revenge the way he wanted to kill Chester Whitcomb for taking the life of a member of his police family.

One life for another was all Ned wanted: Chester Whitcomb's life for Vanessa Conrad's. Being a cop, he wanted that life to be a sentence in state prison. Now that Whitcomb was behind bars, Ned wanted Whitcomb's partner in crime.

With his emotions running so strong, so deep, Ned honestly didn't trust himself to do the right thing, to walk the edge without falling off. He trusted Kenneth, but not one hundred percent, because he couldn't control him. "I'm worried you'll hamper the official police investigation. With the van business and the snitch's tip, we're onto something big when it comes to catching Dr. Thrill. I feel it."

"You and your feelings are what got me involved in the first place."

"True."

"It's also true that it's too late to back down." Kenneth knew every bad guy wasn't all bad, neither was every good guy all good, a rule that applied to himself. He said, "I've got a feeling that if I don't finish this case in the next twenty-four hours, Dr. Thrill will be gone and Daisy might be dead. She feels protected by having Cutie Pie around. But Cutie Pie is a dog. She can only react to her environment. She can't anticipate. I need to stick around Guthrie a little longer."

He spoke the truth when he added, "You were right about one thing. This case is personal now. I've got to see t through to the end."

Ned stared at his friend so long without blinking, the balls of his eyes went dry. He stuck a hand in his pants pocket, pulled a folded sheet of lined white paper from t, then palmed the paper over to Kenneth. The paper showed the address of the strip club Dr. Thrill owned, one of several between Wichita and Guthrie. "Beat it."

Kenneth turned to leave. "Yeah."

A self-contained and proud man, Ned was also ruthless. "I want Dr. Thrill handed to me righteous. No vigilante tuff. We ain't friends when it comes to that. This is business."

Kenneth knew quite well Ned had plenty of clout on

the police force, all of it in good standing, all of it at his instant disposal, which was why none of his threats were idle. But they weren't in Kansas now.

If necessary, their friendship would become a casualty of war. "Yeah," was all Kenneth said.

Daisy and Spud Gurber joined the men. They had been in the house, discussing the case in private while Ned and Kenneth were getting caught up. Mind and body alert, Spud brought along two folding chairs.

"Whether you like it or not, fellas," Daisy said, "I'm involved in this investigation. From what I've pieced together, Chester has killed one woman who crossed him. He could have been on the verge of killing me. He was certainly mad and crazy enough to do it. Bottom line, fellas, is this: I can't stand by and do nothing. It's just not my style. If you're going after this Dr. Thrill character, I want to go, too."

"I just don't want nothing bad to happen to you, girl," Spud said. "Your mama would kill me."

Daisy watched her old friend with neutral eyes, spoke in neutral tones, but didn't fool him one bit. She was bound and determined to stick tight with the ongoing investigation, no matter what happened. "You don't believe I'm thinking straight because I'm involved with Kenneth."

"I don't know the guy, but if you trust him, so do I."

Kenneth grunted. "Go right ahead, folks. Talk about me like I'm not here."

Spud's grin was lopsided, a wolf in policeman's clothing.

Daisy had plenty of experience with Spud, who was busy lighting one of Ned's cigars. She knew he'd been smoking cigars since he was twenty-one, when somebody told him there was less nicotine in a stogie than there was in a regular cigarette. Eyes narrowed, she hissed. "You checked Kenneth out, didn't you?" She threw a thumb in Kenneth's direction.

Spud's face was serious. "You bet I did. That private cop could leave town right now and it wouldn't mean a thing to me, but like I said, your mama would kill me if I let anything happen to ya. How could I know he was who he said he was? I couldn't. Of course I checked him out."

Disgusted, Daisy flopped back in her seat. "Don't you always?"

"Until you get married."

"That sucks."

Spud grinned. "Yep." He took a punch in the shoulder without batting an eye. "Your mama liked to wore my butt out that time I let Charlie Bigelow hold you down for a kiss out on the playground when we was in the fifth grade. She said I know you ain't got no brothers and so I'd better act like I was your brother instead of acting like I didn't have no sense."

Daisy sighed. One of the disadvantages to living in a small town was that some people wouldn't let her grow up. Spud had played big brother for so long, he didn't know when to stop. "I don't need you to protect me."

Kenneth rose to his feet. "That's right," he said. "I'm gonna do it."

Nonchalant, Spud crossed his feet at the ankles. "Not until I've laid some ground rules. Chester is the one guy I didn't check out. I liked him. Because I liked him, I didn't give him the old once-over." He rubbed his hands together. "Now. The ground rules."

Kenneth gave him a like-hell-you-will look. "That won't be necessary," he said.

Spud blew cigar smoke in Kenneth's direction. "Like I said, I've checked you out." He ignored Daisy's groan of dismay. "I know why you quit the force in Wichita."

The private detective glared, but Spud pretended he couldn't see it. "I also know you were and still are highly respected by your old police buddies, Ned Rosa in particular. By the way, Ned. Your credentials are impeccable. But none of that is what sold me on Kenneth here."

Daisy couldn't resist the question. "What did?"

"You, Daisy." Spud locked eyes with Kenneth. "Fact is, your new bodyguard can shoot the feet off a horsefly." Spud's attitude was nonthreatening, but his tone was anything but nice. "She gets hurt, Gunn, even a finger, and I'll spread your butt all over Logan County."

Kenneth's brow returned to its natural position, his glare resolving itself into a normal expression. He no longer looked ready to spit. He sat back. He offered his hand to Spud, the grip firm, the smile on his face tiger-sized and just as deadly.

In that instant, the two men became friends, Daisy the bond between them.

In spite of all the danger, all the intrigue, Daisy never felt so special, or so safe. She laughed. "And people say nothing exciting ever happens in Guthrie."

Daisy grinned in spite of the tense situation. Never in fifty years would she have imagined she'd be spending an evening discussing strategy for chasing down bad guys and fighting crime. She said, "This is great."

With Spud's help, the group put their best plan into action. They made a list of people to talk to about Dr.

Thrill and his possible whereabouts. They would start with Chester's mother and, because they would deal with a woman, Daisy was designated the number-one spokesperson.

Ned said, "I've got to get back to Wichita. Kenneth, keep me informed about whatever you and Daisy find out tomorrow. Spud, we'll be in touch."

Spud stood as well. "Kenneth, you know how I feel about Daisy."

"I do."

"As long as she's happy, I'm happy. Mess up and I'll—"

Daisy slapped his arm. "Spud!"

"—jack you up," he finished.

Kenneth shook hands with Spud. "I hear you."

To Ned, Kenneth said, "I'll call you with a report tomorrow night."

"Deal."

Ned faced Daisy. "Young lady, I think you're tremendous. Thanks for looking out for Kenneth here. He's lucky."

"No problem."

Daisy walked to the house, Cutie Pie at her side. She needed to think, without the distraction of Kenneth, without the cautious scrutiny of Spud, without the calculated stare of Ned Rosa.

Eighteen

The next morning, Daisy took her role as an amateur sleuth seriously, so she noted every detail possible about Mrs. Whitcomb's home once they arrived. A dark blue Mercedes-Benz sedan, circa 1980, took center stage in a driveway flanked by boxwood hedges in serious need of clipping.

The sixty-plus-year-old woman's face was gentle, a little apologetic. She was five feet two inches tall, her salt-and-pepper hair bobbed to the jaw line in a smooth sweep. Her dark pantsuit was strictly Saks Fifth Avenue, as was the ultrafine perfume she wore, a scent that told Daisy Mrs. Whitcomb liked to treat herself well.

It was an admirable trait to take personal pride in body decor, but had Mrs. Whitcomb taken it too far? Had her need to look and feel and live good been the source of Chester's need to sell prescription drugs to Dr. Thrill in order to keep up her facade?

After all, Chester did still live with his mother. Perhaps she knew more than anyone suspected. Daisy made her move to find out.

She spoke through a wrought-iron-and-mesh security screen, painted a robin's egg blue to match the coloring of the one-story, 1950s-style bungalow. "Mrs. Whitcomb, do you know your son's friend, Dr. Thrill?"

"No," the older woman explained. "I'm not around a lot, you know. I work part-time in retail. I volunteer a little at the senior center. That sort of thing. Why are you looking for my son's friend, Daisy? You know full well Chester's in jail because of you. I can't believe you've got the nerve to come to my front door asking questions."

"I'm looking for Dr. Thrill in connection to the murder of Vanessa Conrad. Ever meet her?"

Mrs. Whitcomb fiddled with the scarf draped over her right padded shoulder. Her long nails, filed in perfect ovals, were painted a becoming mauve. The mauve shade matched the lipstick, blush, and eyeshadow on her rum-colored skin. Perfect.

"Of course," she said.

It was the tone of the older woman's voice that arrested Daisy's attention, not the Black Hills gold rings on her fidgety fingers, nor the full carat diamond studs in her ears. Mrs. Whitcomb sounded defensive, her eyes wary.

Daisy asked, "What can you tell me about her?"

Mrs. Whitcomb's fingers stopped moving midstroke, as if she had just become aware she showed her true state of distress. Pampered hands at her sides, she said, "What's to tell? It's none of my business what a grown man does. Is it?"

Kenneth and Daisy had arrived at the front door of the bungalow with the single purpose of digging up clues into Chester's secret lifestyle, not to play nice with his mother, even if playing nice was the polite thing to do.

Daisy ignored the question by asking one of her own.

"What about Chester's brothers and sisters? Could he have taken Vanessa to visit them?"

"None of my children live around here, so that isn't likely," Mrs. Whitcomb said, as cordial as any executive secretary. Professional.

It was her eyes that gave Mrs. Whitcomb away. Something whipped through those sherry-colored eyes, something hot, something so fast it was gone between one blink and the next.

What had she just seen, Daisy wondered. Was it sarcasm? Anger? Deceit? She asked, "Why not?"

Mrs. Whitcomb spoke with total composure. Only the moving door, beginning to close in Daisy's face, showed she realized how many private details she was exposing to unwanted guests on her faded welcome mat; but then, she didn't suffer from ulcers or migraines or any other strong cases of anxiety. Whatever came her way, good or bad, she threw it out in order to let it go. No drama. "My kids aren't all that close," she admitted.

Daisy placed a palm against the security screen, a silent plea for another minute of the petite woman's time. "Mind if I ask you why?"

The door stopped moving, the hand propelling it once more at rest near the woman's side. "Why should I want to talk to you. You're the reason my son is in jail."

"The police have reason to believe Chester killed Vanessa Conrad. There may be other murders committed by him for Dr. Thrill."

"If my son is guilty," Mrs. Whitcomb said, "he should pay. I don't want him to be guilty, though. I want him out of jail. But that doesn't mean I want to involve his friends if they did nothing wrong. You aren't the police, Daisy.

Go home and mind your own business. Let the police find this Dr. Thrill."

"Help us, Mrs. Whitcomb."

"Why?"

"To save other lives."

Mrs. Whitcomb ran her eyes over every centimeter of Daisy's face, nodded her regal head once, sucked a load of air into her lungs, and joined the investigation by being a help instead of a hindrance. "Chester is very neat. Always has been."

She paused, her mind in the past. "As a child, the socks and things in his underwear drawers weren't just tidy, they were in boxes, shoe boxes. All different sizes. Everything had a place and every place was tidy. That was my Chester. Clean. He also liked to *be* clean. Three showers a day weren't too many for him."

Mrs. Whitcomb pursed her lips, her forehead furrowed by the resurrection of memories long forgotten, but remembered now that her son was in so much trouble with the law that it looked as if he might be in jail the rest of his life. Maybe the truth would help him.

She said, "He was always on time. Very organized. With my other kids it was what they did that got them into trouble. But not Chester. No, it was always what Chester said that had me wanting to wring his neck."

She sighed. "I knew that by the time Chester got around to saying whatever it was he had to say, he had been thinking about it for a while and meant it. But I guess what I liked best about Chester was his ambition. Once my son sets his mind to getting something, he always seems to get it. Even if it takes months or even years."

Daisy's gratitude for the elder woman's cooperation

showed through her face and voice. "Why did your son go into the pharmaceutical for hire business?"

"People. Chester was always into figuring out what makes people tick. What makes them do what they do. His being the youngest probably had a hand in that, you know. He was good at reading people, too. He was able to get people to do what he wanted that way, I guess. Manipulative, but smart, too. He was a good boy, my son."

Daisy's heart skipped a beat. "Was?"

"I don't see him much, you know."

"Even though you lived in the same house?" Daisy asked.

"I work. I'm . . . busy." She gazed at a distant point beyond Daisy's head to acknowledge Kenneth. She knew who Kenneth was. Everybody in Guthrie did. "We sort of drifted apart."

The steady ache in the aging, discarded mother's spirit was so tangible, it seeped through the wrought-iron-and-mesh screen of her robin's-egg colored door, breaching the security of Daisy's own emotional distance. She softened her tone. "What about hobbies?"

"Gambling."

This was news to Daisy. "What kind?"

"Horses. He loves the horses, my Chester does."

The woman's eyes, Daisy noticed, had done it again, whipped anew with something hot, something quick, but Daisy had a name now for what she saw: bitterness. "Where did your son do his gambling?"

"The Silver Bucket."

Nineteen

Kenneth rolled Daisy's truck into the parking lot of the Silver Bucket, located in between Guthrie and Langston. One big man and a gorgeous woman snagged a lot of stares, so many stares Kenneth and Daisy never made it through the front door on their own.

With one foot on the top step of the entrance to the Silver Bucket, two thugs grabbed Kenneth.

Daisy recognized them instantly. They were the men who'd attacked her at her garden shop. They were the men in the Ford Econoline van.

The overdressed men patted Kenneth from chest to foot, saw he was not carrying a weapon and hustled them through the front door. One of the thugs made a move for Daisy, a leering look in his eyes.

Kenneth said, "Touch her and I'll break your arm."

The thug took her purse instead.

To keep his eyes focused once he entered the building, Kenneth closed them as he crossed the threshold. He opened them once the door shut behind him. The electric lights inside were dim, but not dim enough to hide the fact that the furnishings inside the club looked worn out.

Sandwiched between Kenneth and the thugs, Daisy felt shock.

Kenneth's face—dark, arrogant, serious—showed every threatening word on his mind about the thugs who refused to let him move forward on his own. The danger in his face was the same that had been shadowing his eyes from the first moment he'd realized Daisy's life was in jeopardy because of his murder investigation. Now this danger had a forum in the Silver Bucket.

The couple were shoved through a door marked PRIVATE.

After the first two thugs made their exit, another two thugs took their places in the private room. One of them said, "Sit."

Kenneth took a seat, but he looked ready to fight on a split second's notice.

Daisy sat, too, and willed her heart to be still. She kept her eyes glued to Kenneth. He was the only one who knew what he was doing, and for the first time since bulldogging her way into his investigation, she felt every bit the wide-eyed amateur.

Kenneth saw her gaze but tuned it out while he took stock of their predicament. He was in a tough situation, a potentially life-threatening one. He had no gun, no back-up, and the woman he loved was looking at him with total trust.

Something deep and primitive moved through Kenneth at the knowledge that Daisy trusted him so completely. He refused to let her down and started counting his assets: his strength, Daisy's courage, and their commitment to getting out of this situation alive.

Kenneth turned his attention outward and faced off with Chester's other employer, Dr. Thrill. He sat behind a fake marble desk, his eyes watchful, his manner unhurried. He was five feet seven inches tall, thin, yellow-skinned, and going bald. Dressed for Wall Street success, the boss man wore a sneer on his face that Kenneth's fist itched to knock off.

Kenneth spoke in a tone that was low and fierce. "We don't have all day."

Ph.D. smart, Dr. Thrill made a living getting cash from gamblers who didn't know when to quit. In his club, people gambled on horses, dogs, cards, and dice. He was open all day and all night. He didn't sell alcohol; he sold drugs he got from Chester Whitcomb. With sex and drugs, Dr. Thrill kept his customers happy.

He also financed multiple high-interest loans, which his customers grabbed with greedy hands, convinced they would strike it big enough to pay off their credit and change their lifestyles.

One big score was all his regular gamblers thought they needed. Dr. Thrill's regular customers were addicted to the services he provided.

Chester had become an addicted man. During the course of his addiction, he had learned to do the unthinkable—to devalue life, his own as well as the lives of the people who loved him the most, the people who kept him from being alone and lonely in the world, people like his mother and Daisy Rogers.

When Dr. Thrill told Chester to kill Vanessa Conrad, Chester had done it. Being with Daisy helped him pretend he wasn't a bad guy after all. Being with Daisy kept Chester sane, until Kenneth came along.

Dr. Thrill wanted Kenneth and Daisy to squirm. As they watched him, he studied the Daily Racing Form in his hand, the undisputed record of every recent race for every horse on the racing card scheduled to run on any given day at the Remington racetrack. He enjoyed reading the charts showing which horse was scheduled to race versus which horse was scheduled to just work out.

All the abbreviations, each devised of numbers and letters, comprised a foreign language he loved to speak and hear. In a stack on a nearby table were racetrack programs, his tools for knowing about a specific race when it came to betting.

From the racetrack program, he found out a key horse's distance record, the length of the race, the total purse being paid to winners, the horse's position number, the jockey's name, the owner's name, as well as details about the running racehorse.

More than anything, he liked watching races live. Wearing binoculars to follow his favorite horse and jockey around the track was exhilarating, far better than watching it from a big screen in the smoke-filled lounge at the Silver Bucket.

Monitor viewing lost the spectacular details of horses leaving their paddocks, horses stretching their bodies in warm-up drills, horses racing, then cooling down before returning to their paddocks.

Dr. Thrill thought about Chester, a man who loved to bet on the Daily Double, the Daily Triple, the Pick Six, and the Trifecta.

The Trifecta was Chester's downfall. To repay the money he owed, he distributed prescription drugs to Dr. Thrill's clients.

Dr. Thrill believed Chester failed at the races because he seldom got around to the tracks in person, preferring the off-track betting sites with the big television screens and big talkers, not understanding the ultrafine points of horse betting: knowing the class and condition of a horse and the daily physical conditions of the track.

He was lousy at budgeting, which was why he borrowed money from Dr. Thrill at ridiculous rates of interest. Chester made mistakes managing his money; Dr. Thrill did not. Chester's mistakes made him desperate.

Because Dr. Thrill had refined his money management to a science, he was able to attend the great races when he wanted to be there: the Belmont, the Preakness, the Breeders' Cup Classic, the Kentucky Derby. He had been to the best racing tracks in the United States, from the oldest one at Churchill Downs in Kentucky, to the newest one at Remington Park in Oklahoma.

Suckers, like Chester, paved Dr. Thrill's way to the good life, a life filled with excitement and material things, blood and money, thousands of dollars in cash and hard assets. Only Chester was messing it all up. By choosing the wrong woman to fall in love with—Daisy—then by choosing the wrong kind of men for friends, opportunistic men like Harold.

Dr. Thrill turned his mind away from his horse-racing paraphernalia. He did it cleanly with the certain knowledge that no man would take from him what he felt he deserved. He deserved to maintain his current lifestyle.

Using no words, just a slight nod of his head, Dr. Thrill told the largest thug to do his bidding. The thug took one thick hand, opened it up, and smacked Kenneth flat across his pissed-off face. He smacked him so hard, Kenneth's chair rocked back like a dog on its hind legs.

Dr. Thrill said, "That was your only warning."

Kenneth kept his cool, but it wasn't easy. He settled his chair back on the gray carpeted floor, spread his legs wide, and acted as if his bottom lip wasn't split. He ignored Daisy's gasp of surprise in order to concentrate on their common and immediate enemies. He had thought Daisy would be safer with him but he was wrong.

Dr. Thrill cracked his knuckles and the silence, too. "You've got guts."

Kenneth sat easy in his chair. His face throbbed, his ears buzzed, but he ignored the pain, his mind focused on the investigation. He didn't want Daisy to be afraid, so he kept his face cold, hard, fearless.

Daisy couldn't believe Kenneth's bold attitude against Dr. Thrill and his henchmen. On this day, she had seen him go from gentle, kind, and considerate to absolutely fearless. For her, the transition was stunning.

Until now, she had viewed his work as minimum-risk. She had envisioned him as sort of a well-dressed Columbo, the kind of detective who never shot a bullet, instead using his mind to outwit and capture the number-one suspect.

Columbo always had just one suspect in mind, the way Kenneth did, but unlike Columbo, Kenneth wasn't truly low key. His quiet, investigative demeanor was merely camouflage. Effective camouflage, because he'd certainly had her fooled.

Watching him get his face backhanded by Dr. Thrill's bodyguard gave her chills. This was no mild-mannered Columbo she'd been dealing with all along, it was Spenser, the hard-loving, soft-hearted knight in flesh and blood— and he was all hers. She caught his eye, her admiration stamped indelibly on her face.

Kenneth told Dr. Thrill, "You have to let us go."

"Why?"

"Ned Rosa from Wichita PD knows about you. So does Spud Gurber of the Guthrie PD. Something happens to me or Daisy and you're a dead man."

Dr. Thrill had been born with an excellent poker face. "The Silver Bucket is a legal establishment. You won't connect me or my sister to murder."

"Your sister?" Kenneth said.

"Yes. She's the woman Chester thinks you saw in Guthrie. She . . . handles some business details for me."

"You mean she transfers prescription drugs between you and Chester."

"I don't know what you mean. The police have no evidence to connect me with any crime. If you could find me, they could too. I think you're here to rattle me in some way. I don't sell drugs and I don't kill people. Chester is the guilty one."

"Eventually you'll make a mistake."

Dr. Thrill laughed. The sound of it was harsh. "I'm not worried and I won't make any bogus confessions."

For Kenneth, there was no need for more violence. He'd found Dr. Thrill for Ned. He'd found out who the mystery woman was. Now it was time to get Daisy home, safe.

He said in a low, hoarse voice, "We're leaving. Get in my way, and we'll all be sorry."

Kenneth left the Silver Bucket, his strides long and direct, his sidekick, Daisy, beside him as if they always had and always would work together.

Despite the dire circumstances that brought the two of them together, Kenneth felt alive and utterly unstoppable. He was in love. The love filled him with power, the absolute faith that good would triumph over evil. He had no idea that it was this absolute faith in all things good that had won Daisy's heart for him.

Justice had been served to Vanessa Conrad's killer, Chester Whitcomb. Without a confession or solid evidence, Dr. Thrill would not be indicted for any crime. It wasn't fair but Kenneth knew that in real life, sometimes killers or their accomplices got away with murder.

From now on, Dr. Thrill would be looking over his shoulder. If Kenneth found him once, he'd find him again.

Epilogue

The scent of sex eased through the still air inside Daisy's bedroom where she lay, feeling spent and delicious, in the tender arms of her rogue lover. It had been three months since the Vanessa Conrad case had been closed.

"The answer is no, Kenneth. If we move in together, we'll get caught up in some kind of routine that will change how we deal with each other everyday. I like the way things stand between us right now."

He bit her bottom lip. "And how is that?"

"All hot and loose and free."

He flexed the muscle of one thigh against her. He stroked her hip, the gentle move of his fingers easing her muscles into smooth lines, the slight touch of his nails brushing her skin until she shimmied in soft waves of desire. "If we lived together, Daisy, we could make love like this every morning."

His low, raspy voice turned her body heat from simmer to medium high. In response to this rise in body temperature, she cupped Kenneth's face in her hands, the texture of his skin rough and warm beneath the flesh of her palms.

Snuggling up close to the hard length of him, Daisy pressed her mouth to Kenneth's, then slowly, gently, she eased her tongue over the firm line that separated his top lip from his bottom.

Her voice was husky when she said, "I cherish being single and I cherish our relationship. Call me greedy, but I want to keep living separate but shared lives. I mean, I already know I'm not cut out for the dinner-on-the-table-by-five routine, so why screw things up trying to be somebody I'm not meant to be?"

He sounded thoughtful. "So you propose a sort of . . . Susan Silverman and Spenser–style relationship?"

Her eyes lit up at the mention of Robert Parker's crime fighting characters. "It's almost the perfect solution."

"Almost?"

"You want a wife."

"I want you."

Her voice was grave. "What about children?"

"I've thought a lot about them. We both work six days a week, sometimes at twelve-hour stretches a day. Raising a family would mean we'd have to cut back. Since we run our own businesses, that isn't a practical choice. I love children, Daisy, but I don't need them in order to be happy. I'm happy right now, but you, how do you feel about kids?"

"When I get motherly cravings I keep my sister's children for the weekend. This might sound cold and heartless, but borrowing my niece and nephew a few days at a time is enough for me. Besides, there's always Cutie Pie."

Kenneth nuzzled Daisy's collarbone. "Another similarity between Susan and Spenser," he murmured. "They have a pet they share together."

Daisy sighed. "I know a pet is nothing like having a child, but it gives us a common responsibility."

"I hear you and I agree, but in the long run, will sharing a pet be enough for you?"

"For now, the answer is yes. I'm happy with my life the way it is. To tell you the truth, Kenneth, I think it's more likely for you to change your mind about parenthood than it is for me. I distinctly remember you telling me once that you want a station wagon full of screaming kids."

"That was then, this is now. When I first left the police force, I discovered that some of what I thought I wanted wasn't what I wanted after all. So, to tell *you* the truth, if I'd gone for the station wagon, I'd have been bored out of my mind at some point. I've lived a dangerous lifestyle for too long not to miss the adrenaline rush I get sometimes walking on the dark side. You give me a rush and you're safe."

Daisy kissed him. "The best of both worlds."

"Yeah, except for one thing."

"What?"

"Monogamy."

She snorted. "I pity the woman who tries to take my place."

Her jealous nature thrilled him. "Is that right?

"You better believe it when I tell you that somebody would have to scrape her silly butt off the floor when I got done with her."

Chuckling low in his throat, Kenneth raised his torso by resting his body on one elbow so that his view of her face was clear. "What sharp claws you have, pretty kitty."

"You better believe it buddy, because when I finished

picking her hair off my fingers, I'd go after you." When his low chuckle turned into a full-bodied laugh, she nipped his ear, licked the bite, then whispered, "You belong to me now, just like I belong to you."

Fierce, bold eyes traveled over her face before meeting her gaze in a silent exchange of vows, solemn pledges of faith that were as old and everlasting as eternity. "Sexy, eccentric, ambitious, bloodthirsty. No wonder everything I thought I wanted changed the day I met you. I love you, Daisy Rogers. Only you."

Rolling him onto his back, she conformed the supple curves of her body to the broad line of his heavy frame. Reveling in her sole possession of the most dynamic man she had ever known, Daisy said sincerely, "I love you too, Kenneth Gunn."

Dear Readers:

Simply Wonderful is not a true story. However, the City of Guthrie does actually exist. Guthrie is a small historic town in Oklahoma and is famous for being the largest city of original Victorian buildings in this country. Guthrie is also the site of the last American Land Rush, an event that occurred in April 1889.

Any mistakes that were made about law enforcement or any place of business in Oklahoma or Kansas are my errors alone. If you live in Guthrie, I hope you will look at the familiar places featured in this story with a fresh eye and a feeling of pride.

I'd love to hear your comments about *Simply Wonderful*. Please feel free to write me at P.O. Box 253, Guthrie, Oklahoma, 73044, and be sure to include an SASE. It may take a while, but I do answer every letter I receive.

Currently, I am working on another Sam and Bailey Walker story. It's called *Sacred Love* and will be in stores in August 2001.

Best wishes to you all,
Shelby Lewis

COMING IN JANUARY FROM
ARABESQUE ROMANCES

__PRIVATE PASSIONS

by Rochelle Alers   1-58314-151-0 $5.99US/$7.99CAN

Successful journalist Emily Kirkland never expected that her long-time friendship with gubernatorial candidate Christopher Delgado would ignite a dangerously irresistible desire—and result in their secret marriage. Now, with scandal and a formidable enemy threatening all of their most cherished dreams, Emily must uncover the truth, risking all for a passion that could promise forever . . .

__A SECOND CHANCE AT LOVE

by Janice Sims   1-58314-153-7 $5.99US/$7.99CAN

Author Toni Shaw has it all: two grown daughters on their own, a hot new novel in stores, and a gorgeous man in her bed. It's been three years since the father of her children entered her life, and things between Toni and Charles Waters are better than ever—until he pops an unexpected question: Will you marry me?

__GOOD INTENTIONS

by Crystal Wilson-Harris   1-58314-154-5 $5.99US/$7.99CAN

Minutes before she was about to marry Chicago's most-desirable catch, bride-to-be Ivy Daniels realized she needed time to sort out what *she* really wanted. With the unexpected help of handsome stranger Ben Stephens, she promptly bolts the "wedding-of-the-year"—only to discover a scandalous, surprising passion.

__TRULY

by Adrienne Ellis Reeves, Geri Guillaume, Mildred Riley
                    1-58314-196-0 $5.99US/$7.99CAN

It is a day of hearts by surprise—and promises forever kept. Spend a glorious Valentine's Day with three of Arabesque's best loved authors and discover love's most passionate delights.

Call toll free **1-888-345-BOOK** to order by phone or use this coupon to order by mail. *ALL BOOKS AVAILABLE JANUARY 1, 2001.*

Name_____

Address _____

City _____ State _____ Zip _____

Please send me the books I have checked above.

I am enclosing $_____
Plus postage and handling* $_____
Sales tax (+in NY and TN) $_____
Total amount enclosed $_____

*Add $2.50 for the first book and $.50 for each additional book.

Send check or money order (no cash or CODs) to:

Kensington Publishing Corp., Dept. C.O., 850 Third Avenue, New York, NY 10022

Prices and numbers subject to change without notice. Valid only in the U.S. All orders subject to availability. **NO ADVANCE ORDERS.**

Visit our website at **www.arabesquebooks.com.**

Arabesque Romances
by *Roberta Gayle*